PUBLIC LIBRARY
Hamilton, MA 01982
9/2 0

THE ELUSIVE SHADOWS

Brian Stableford's scholarly work includes *New Atlantis: A Narrative History of Scientific Romance* (Wildside Press, 2016), *The Plurality of Imaginary Worlds: The Evolution of French roman scientifique* (Black Coat Press, 2017) and *Tales of Enchantment and Disenchantment: A History of Faerie* (Black Coat Press, 2019). In support of the latter projects he has translated more than a hundred volumes of *roman scientifique* and more than twenty volumes of *contes de fées* into English. He has edited *Decadence and Symbolism: A Showcase Anthology* (Snuggly Books, 2018), and is busy translating more Symbolist and Decadent fiction.

His recent fiction, in the genre of metaphysical fantasy, includes a trilogy of novels set in West Wales, consisting of *Spirits of the Vasty Deep* (2018), *The Insubstantial Pageant* (2018) and *The Truths of Darkness* (2019), published by Snuggly Books; and a trilogy set in Paris and the south of France, consisting of *The Painter of Spirits*, *The Quiet Dead* and *Living with the Dead*, all published by Black Coat Press in 2019; and the futuristic fantasy *The Revelations of Time and Space* (Snuggly Books 2020).

D1593498

SNUGGLY
BOOKS

BRIAN STABLEFORD

THE
ELUSIVE
SHADOWS

A TALE OF THE BIOTECH REVOLUTION

THIS IS A SNUGGLY BOOK

Copyright © 2020 by Brian Stableford.
All rights reserved.

ISBN: 978-1-64525-051-7

THE
ELUSIVE
SHADOWS

1

When Adrian told his PhD supervisor, Professor Artemus Clark, that he had been invited to the Savoy the following day to meet Jason Jarndyke, the professor raised an eyebrow, and adopted a quizzical expression, as if he didn't know whether to beam with polite delight or sigh with unjustified disappointment. As a career academic, he tended to assume that his star pupils ought to follow him into academe, especially if they seemed to him to be as ill-equipped for what he was wont to refer to as "the harsh and dreary world of industry" as Adrian.

After a few seconds, though, he settled for an absurdly neutral comment. "They didn't ask me for a reference," he observed.

In the world of academe, personal references were still very much *de rigeur*, but Jason Jarndyke, despite the fact that he made such a song and dance about the great tradition of the Yorkshire textile industry, was a very modern man. He didn't advertise positions in his Research and Development Division. He employed headhunters to identify the people best-suited to the jobs he needed done, and then he contacted them. He always handled the approach himself, unwilling to employ anyone in a position that might be important to the profitability of his enterprise without a personal inspection.

After another few seconds, perhaps suspecting that his utterly innocuous remark might have given the wrong impression, the professor added: "If they had, of course, it would have been glowing." He attempted a smile, as if it qualified as a joke to give an expert in color biochemistry a glowing reference—especially an oddball like Adrian, who was undoubtedly the only person in his field in England, and perhaps in the world, to combine an expertise in esoteric biochemistry with a strong interest in the esthetics of color.

"Thanks," said Adrian, reflexively. "I really think that it's a perfect opportunity for me—something I've been expecting, to tell you the truth, but hadn't dared to bank on until the call came. I only hope that I don't mess up the interview. I really want the job."

Briefly, the professor's time-worn face took on the expression of a man who had just found half a caterpillar in his apple, but he controlled it swiftly. "If you think so," he said, his tone implying involuntarily that no sane man would. "You'll be finishing up here, though, first? You still have six months of lab time in hand."

Adrian had submitted his thesis already, and it had been approved, although he couldn't actually graduate until July. However, he had continued working in the labs and had a dozen experiments in progress, at various stages, in which his supervisor still had an academic interest and the university still had a proprietary interest—a not inconsiderable one, since he had already clocked up a record number of patents for a PhD student in the course of the last three-and-a-half years.

"I don't know exactly how it will work, if Jarndyke does offer me a job," Adrian said, "but I gather that he likes to move quickly. He'll probably want to transfer my work in progress to his own labs, and pay the university a transfer fee for the latent commercial value."

The professor made a show of shuffling papers on his desk. Clark always had papers on his desk, in considerable quantities and ostentatious disorder. He had been born in the twentieth century and although the web era had been well advanced by the time he did his own PhD, he had not escaped the hangover of traditional technological inertia. He had been a pioneer in his day, but now he was a dinosaur. The pace of change in applied genomics during his adulthood had been steady enough, but had added up to a considerable total over nearly fifty years. He showed his age even more in his manner than his gray hair and wrinkles.

"Transfer fee!" he muttered. "In my day, only footballers had transfer fees. And as for latent commercial value . . . well, accountants hadn't even come up with that kind of arithmetic yet. Intellectual property still meant books, with actual pages, made of wood-pulp."

Adrian knew enough history to know that he was exaggerating. Books with wood-pulp pages had been on the way out while the commercial value of Professor

Clark's work was still latent and not yet conventionally calculable.

"At any rate, Professor," he said, "it's possible that the next time I see you will just be to say goodbye. I thought I ought to let you know." He was about to go on to say, politely if not entirely sincerely, that it had been a pleasure and a privilege working under the professor's supervision, and then slip away, but now that he'd been warned, Artemus Clark wanted at least to raise a token protest. Like many people of his generation, sixty per cent of his conversation consisted of complaining that the world had gone horribly wrong since "his day"—which in view of the ongoing eco-catastrophe, was impossible to deny in a general sense, although Adrian liked to think of applied genomics as shining beacon of light in the darkness, and a viable route to the salvation of civilized society, art, beauty and everything else that was good and worthwhile.

"But you have real talent, damn it!" the professor said, in a slightly agonized tone, as if he were the victim of a treason. "You've worked so hard—too hard, some might say, although I've never thought there was any such thing—and come so far in a mere three years. You're a real scientist, not just someone who's learning the trade so that he can qualify for a salary and perks doing DNA-cookery in some short-order kitchen. With your intelligence and imagination, you could do *anything*. Why on earth do you want to settle for *coloring textiles?*"

Adrian knew that his supervisor was exaggerating in saying that he could do "anything," but not by that much. What the jargon of mass reportage had taken to calling "reverse genetic engineering," had an enormous potential range of applications, in the fields of artificial photosynthesis, atmospheric management, bioelectricity, medicine, food technology, etcetera, etcetera. By comparison with some of those fields, in which heroic laborers could legitimately claim to be saving the planet and paving the way for a better posthumanity, the textile industry seemed a trifle pedestrian.

Even without abandoning his intense interest in the genetics and esthetics of color, and his desire to quit the groves of academe, Adrian could easily have found other industries in which potential employers would be eager to employ him. The combination of genetics and esthetics would certainly not have been irrelevant to food technology, for instance. Although the occasionally-voiced suspicion that he was borderline anorectic was unjustified, Adrian found food essentially uninteresting, regarding it as mere fuel for the flesh. Textiles, on the other hand, were the raw material of the fashion industry and the eye-candy business. Eccentric as it would doubtless have seemed to the professor, if Adrian had made a serious attempt to explain it to him, the textile industry was the perfect arena for testing certain hypotheses dear to Adrian's offbeat intellect, and perhaps proving, at least to himself, that he was not suffering from a nexus of deep-seated delusions. From his point of view, the invitation to meet Jason Jarndyke was a godsend, the kind of opportunity that might only knock once in a lifetime, or not at all.

There were, however, things that he could not explain to Professor Clark. He had confided a part of his great secret to him, but by no means all of it. Indeed, he had deliberately understated the extent of his ability, in the interests of seeming as close to normal as possible, while still conserving his claim to be able to do something that most people could not. It was, he had decided long ago, the safest course. Given that he was regarded as a "biogeek" anyway, because of his purely intellectual interests, and as a "semi-autistic social retard" because he was so narrowly focused on those intellectual interests, the addition of an extra dimension of freakishness did not seem out of place, provided that it was something moderate and seemingly harmless. There was a point, however, at which the scope of his claims would overstep what too many commonplace individuals considered to be the borderline of madness, and Adrian was always very careful not to test that frontier of credulity to destruction.

"Given that my field of specialization is the genetics of pigmentation," he contented himself with saying, "the textile industry is the natural place for me to go. After all, the reason natural selection developed pigmentation so extensively was for the purposes of natural clothing, in flowers, in the plumage of birds and the wings of butterflies."

"You mean sexual display," Clark corrected him, a trifle testily. He was not a handsome man, and both his marriages had ended in divorce, souring his attitude.

"Clothing has more than one function," Adrian said, mildly, "and that makes for interesting interactions between color and texture, beauty, comfort and warmth. That complexity of function is vital to the esthetics of fabrics and garments . . . which is one of my principal interests."

"Well, there aren't many genetic engineers addicted to art galleries, it's true," Clark conceded. "But Jason Jardyke? A professional Yorkshireman with a trophy wife. Is a flashy entrepreneur of his sort really the kind of man you want to work for?"

"Yes it is," said Adrian, positively. "A flashy entrepreneur, as you put it, is exactly the kind of employer I need: energetic, determined, the very opposite of risk averse. His media image is undoubtedly something of a caricature, but it implies that he's the kind of man who will not only give me scope to develop my offbeat theories, but actively encourage me to do so and put the results to a proper test. The newsfeeds are just making silly jokes when they talk about the Airedale Argonaut and the new quest for the Golden Fleece—but I can make that dream a reality. I might look puny and a trifle pasty-faced, but I can be the Hercules of his *Argo*, if he'll give me the chance."

The professor opened his mouth to make a further objection, but Adrian didn't want to waste any more time. He stood up, albeit with slight difficulty, because the professor preferred to set his students in low armchairs, while retaining one with a higher seat for himself, behind the rampart of his desk and his paper crenellations.

"Anyway, Professor," Adrian said, in what he hoped was a suitably businesslike fashion, "if it goes well, things will probably move swiftly. I just wanted to tell you, in case I don't get another chance, that it's been a pleasure and a privilege working with you these last three-and-a-half years. You've taught me a lot, and you've been very tolerant of my . . . eccentric interests. I'm very grateful to you for that."

That took the wind out of the sails of complaint. Professor Clark even blushed slightly, appreciating the flattery. "There's no genius in orthodoxy," he said—one of his numerous pet phrases. "Discovery comes from thinking outside the box and putting ideas together that no one ever thought of combining before." He could not help adding, though: "On the other hand, it's a way of going about things that sometimes produces nothing but chimeras."

"There's no gain without risk," Adrian said, figuring that if a man of Artemus Clark's intellectual stature and bizarre nomenclature could stoop to commonplace cliché, there was no reason why his soon-to-be-ex-student, a mere Adrian, couldn't do likewise.

He almost managed to turn away and make for the door, but the professor wasn't quite ready to let go.

"Does working in the textile industry, in the dark satanic mils of Yorkshire, really qualify as *risk?*" he queried. "Don't you think you might find the routines of factory work a trifle dull?" The ghost of a wry smile crossed his face, as he realized that his use of the word dull, offered as a challenge to an expert on color, might qualify as wordplay much as his earlier reference to a glowing reference might have done.

Adrian, who was highly literate by comparison with most of the postgraduates in the Applied Genomics department, was tempted to inform him that some critics thought that William Blake's reference to dark satanic mills in "Jerusalem" was metaphorical, referring to universities rather than actual mills, but he refrained. If this really was the terminus of his official relationship with the representative of academe, he didn't want to end it on a sour note.

"I honestly don't think I'll find it dull," Adrian assured him. "To the man in the street, here in London as well as in Yorkshire, all lab work seems dull and tedious—just men in white coats playing with liquids and gels in flasks and Petri dishes . . . or, given the way that forensic science TV detective shows have educated the popular imagination for half a century and more, decoding cryptic graphs spewed out by mass spectrometers and blurred spectra from sequencers. You and I know where the real drama lies. I'll have plenty to occupy my intellect and my curiosity. As for risk . . . yes, it really does qualify as risk." *A hell of a lot more so than university teaching*, he carefully refrained from adding.

Artemus Clark, of course, had no idea what kind of risk it was, or what was at stake. Adrian had been tempted, once or twice, in spite of the once-bitten-twice-shy principle, to explain to his supervisor more fully why he was so very interested in the phenomenon of color, but while the professor had some authority over his destiny, he had maintained his prudence sternly. It was strategically necessary to feign a safe degree of normality, even with a man who had been stuck

15

by his parents with a name like Artemus, for reasons that remained stubbornly obscure. Popular speculation suggested that it was because his father couldn't spell Artemis and didn't realize that it was the name of a goddess, not a god, but Adrian never took rumors of that glib variety seriously.

"Well," said the professor, finally standing up in his turn, presumably deciding that he too ought to play normal, or at least to pretend to be polite, "if it's what you want, I wish you the very best of luck. I don't know anything about Jarndyke except for his media profile, and I assume that all his song and dance about the economic regeneration of the North and reclaiming the revolutionary heritage of Yorkshire industry is mostly PR bluster, but he certainly seems to be energetic and enterprising, as you say. If he does ask for a belated reference, I'll be glad to confirm that you're at the very top of your field, and that while applied genomics is bringing about a revolution in the textile industry, there's no one better to take the reins of that revolution than you. I'll be careful not to compare you to Robespierre, in spite of the opportunity to make jokes about sea-green incorruptibility."

"Thanks," said Adrian. "I appreciate it." And he did appreciate it, even though he was convinced that he was already well past the point at which he needed that kind of recommendation, with or without the silly wordplay.

He knew little more about Jason Jarndyke than Professor Clark did, having derived it from exactly the same corrupt sources, but he was prepared to assume that the Yorkshireman's media profile was as misleading as all media profiles seemed to be to the skeptical eye. On the other hand, Adrian thought, even if Jarndyke really were what popular speculation considered him to be, all was not lost by any means. He was convinced that he could make Jason Jarndyke money—*lots* of money—by means of the application of his unique combination of talents, even though his real objectives lay far beyond that. It *was* a risk, and he might be wrong, but it was not only a risk worth taking, but a risk he felt that he had to take, if he was ever to prove himself to himself.

What might happen if he did manage to prove himself, and establish his sanity beyond reasonable doubt, he was not sure. At present, that was still a vague prospect in more ways than one, but for the time being, he saw it as an end rather than a means, and if the side-effects of achieving that end included making truckloads of money for Jason Jarndyke, that was all to the good. Crass or not, Jarndyke was a man whose business did no one any harm. He was on the side of the angels. And getting a good and secure job in a field where his particular expertise could be applied in interesting ways was a vital first step on the road to any future for which he might care to aim. Once that base was secure, other possibilities would become visible, with the all the myriad blues of the sky to tempt and guide him.

Everything would be rosy—with the possible exception of the elusive shadows.

But for the moment, Adrian did not want to think about the elusive shadows. They were a problem of an entirely different order, in personal as well as philosophical terms.

Artemus Clark moved around his desk, slightly uncomfortably, in order to shake Adrian's hand. He did—but he was a little slow in letting go, as if there were something on his mind that wanted to say but thought it might be better not to express. He was, however, not a man to resist temptation for long.

"It could be an awkward interview," he observed. "As I say, I only know Jarndyke through the media, but . . . well, the words chalk and cheese do come to mind."

"It's a challenge," Adrian admitted, "but there's no point in trying to pretend to be what I'm not and putting on an act. He's looking for a scientist, after all, not a PR man. If he finds me a trifle . . . introverted . . . he surely won't consider that inappropriate to the kind of job he wants me to do. He's obviously prepared to overlook the fact that I was born and bred in Sussex."

His supervisor nodded. "You're probably right," he said, with blatant insincerity.

If the professor seemed dubious, Adrian thought, it was probably because he was very conscious of the fact that he did not "interview well" in a conventional sense himself.

"Actually," Adrian said, not sure whether it was the truth, "I'm not that nervous. It won't be the kind of interview that requires an image-consultant's notion of selling myself. If he's doing it himself, it's because he wants to cut through the stereotyped HR bullshit. All I have to do it set out what I might be able to do for him, to confirm what his headhunters have already told him. It really is exactly what he needs. If he were to be put off by my appearance or manner . . . well, he wouldn't be the kind of person I could work for."

That was not the point that the professor had been trying to make. "There's nothing wrong with your appearance, and you talk exceptionally well, for a biogeek," he said. "There's no danger there—but don't you think that your theories might sound a little . . . well, *far out?*"

You have no idea, my dear innocent Professor, how far out some of my hypotheses really are, Adrian thought. What he said aloud was: "My bet is that that's exactly what he's looking for. If his headhunters have researched me thoroughly—*all* my publications—he knows full well that I have original and unusual ideas. That's surely what he wants. I'll wear a suit and tie, just to show willing, but that's as far as I'll go in the direction of convention."

"I didn't know you possessed a suit and tie," the professor commented, trying with a half-smile to make the dig sound like the kind of amicable remark that friends might exchange.

"Everybody has to go to funerals occasionally," Adrian retorted. "My mother would never have forgiven me if I'd turned up to my father's in a T-shirt and jeans. You don't do that in Sussex, even nowadays—nor in Yorkshire, I suspect. And I inherited my father's old ties, so I have half a dozen that aren't black. Unfortunately, he was a much larger size than me, so all his suits went to the local charity shop."

"How will your mother feel about you relocating to Yorkshire, if you get the job?" It was the first time in three and a half years that Artemus Clark had ever inquired about Adrian's mother or any aspect of his life outside the laboratory and the seminar room.

"She'll complain," Adrian admitted, itching to reach out for the door handle but unable to tear himself away while the professor was suffering a belated fit of camaraderie. "But that's good. If it weren't for things to complain about, she'd have no conversation at all. Anyway, since my sister got a job in Sweden, she's had to learn to use Skype, and given the dilapidated state of the roads and railways, even the distance between Brighton and London isn't trivial. She's adapted well enough to widowhood not to need her children close at hand."

All of that was of no interest at all to the professor, but he was a stubborn man, and he still wasn't ready to let go

"And you really think that you can convince Jason Jardyke that innate pigmentation will make a significant difference to his bottom line?"

"I'm convinced that I won't have to. If he wasn't already convinced, he wouldn't be entertaining me to tea at the Savoy. But if he does have any hesitation, I'm sure I can tip the balance. It's the way his industry has to go, and if he wants to be in the van, he needs someone who can steer it in that direction. In the eyes of a dynamic professional Yorkshireman, I might look like an effete southerner, but I'm also the only man in

England, perhaps in the world, who can give him what he needs right now."

"Well, in that case," said Professor Clark, finally settling for a sigh of farewell, "I suppose the only useful advice I can give you is to watch out for Medea."

"Who's Medea?" Adrian asked, with a hint of embarrassment. He did not like to be caught out by his supervisor's allusions, although it was occasionally inevitable, given his relative youth and the professor's relative antiquity.

Artemus Clark raised his eyes to the heavens, miming despair, although Adrian suspected that he was secretly delighted to score the point. All serious scientists cultivated some area of humanistic interest in order to deflect of suspicion of terminal dullness, and Clark was proud of his acquaintance with the classics. Adrian had too many idiosyncratic interests of his own to have made any attempt to catch up with him on that ground. "Jason's wife," the professor said, with mock weariness. "The newsfeeds haven't taken it up yet, but it's only a matter of time."

Adrian was able to get the gist of the suggestion, although he knew that he would have to use a search engine to find out exactly what crimes the mythical Medea was supposed to have committed, if he could be bothered—but he couldn't prevent himself from putting on a mock-ingenuous expression and replying: "I think Mrs. Jarndyke's name is Angelica." He had no definite knowledge, but presumed that she must be an effete southerner too. Even in this day and age, surely no one in Yorkshire would ever have named a girl Angelica.

The professor sighed again, and muttered something to himself that might or might not have been a reference to "lamb to the slaughter"—which, in turn, might or might not have been an attempt at a witty play on words based on the fact that half of Jason Jarndyke's most profitable mills produced wool by the mile, without the necessity of employing actual sheep. The other half produced silk, without the need for worms.

Supervisor and student finally parted, if not quite on the best of terms, on terms as good as could be expected. The second and final handshake, on the threshold of the office, had a certain amount of sincere warmth, although the promises to keep in touch offered in either side were evidently false.

2

Unsurprisingly, Jason Jarndyke did not seem to be nearly as extravagant in person as the more scurrilous newsfeeds painted him, and Adrian scolded himself for being slightly surprised by that, having unconsciously fallen victim to web-spun prejudice in spite of knowing better.

Jarndyke was a big man, to be sure, with rather coarse features, and he spoke with a broad Yorkshire accent—which had become rare, except as deliberate affectation, since a century of saturation exposure to TV had begun smoothing all regional dialects into subtlety—but he had a definite charm and a casual joviality that worked far better in the flesh than on screen. Once he had been in the man's company for half an hour, moreover, Adrian was fully convinced that Jarndyke's accent was no mere affectation, and that his renowned bluntness was also perfectly natural—or, at least, not mere rudeness with a tacit apology in tow. Jason Jarndyke gave every sign of being honest, sincere—and intelligent.

The textile-manufacturer didn't get down to business right away. For a while, they nibbled sandwiches, ate cake and drank tea—the Savoy was very proud of its adherence to tradition in the matter of teas—and chatted. Unlike Artemus Clark, Jarndyke enquired right away about the health of Adrian's mother, his sister's employment in Sweden, and the colossal advantage that Imperial College had in being so close to the V&A and only a short walk from the Royal Academy and the National Gallery.

"Do you like art galleries yourself, then?" Adrian asked—because he was interested, not became he was desperate for conversational fodder.

"Personally, not so much," Jarndyke admitted, "but Angie—that's my wife—loves them. Wherever we go, we have to take in the local art. She was at the Courtauld for a while before she went into serious modeling and had to drop her studies. Always regretted it, I think. But I'm here to quiz you, not to talk about me and mine. I see from your CV that you've published papers on esthetics as well as genetic engineering—the legacy of your interesting in painting, no doubt—and also on the subliminal psychological effects of color."

"They're not really papers," Adrian said. "Just articles, more speculation than science. The kind of jottings with which the cloud is bulging nowadays. I'd be surprised if more than half a dozen people have read them—and astonished if your headhunters bothered."

Jarndyke laughed. "Well, I haven't read them," he condeded. "I'll get Angie to take a look, though—that's a promise. Give you something to talk about when you meet her."

Adrian was making every effort to maintain his customary impassive expression, but he assumed that his eyebrows must have lifted slightly, because Jarndyke said: "Oh, don't pretend to be surprised, Son. You know as well as I do that we wouldn't be here if I weren't going to offer you a job. I'm only trying to figure out exactly how much you're worth and make sure that I can outbid whatever the competition have offered you."

"Actually," Adrian admitted, although he knew that it might be reckoned a poor move tactically, "the opposition haven't offered me anything. You seem to be the only interested party, thus far."

"Well, I like to be at the head of the queue. Strategy is getting there firstest with the mostest men, isn't that what they say? Except, in business, it's getting there firstest with the mostest cash. My spies have already weighed up what they think you're worth in cash terms, but I like to know what a man's worth in other terms too—because, contrary to popular opinion, business isn't just about money . . . or, if it is, being *about money* is a lot more complicated than most people think. Making it is a matter of building a strong team, who can play together effectively. It's not just arithmetic. So you'll forgive me, won't you, for wanting to know more about you . . . and for wanting you to know more about me. I don't want you to regard working for Jarkdyke Industries as a step on some career ladder that will just give you a way to move on. It's my life, and if I think you'll fit into it, I'd try to make it worth your while for it to be your life too."

Adrian had already noticed that Jason Jarndyke wasn't addressing him as "Mr. Stamford," in the same way that he was addressing his prospective employer as "Mr. Jarndyke," but he realized that addressing him as "Son" wasn't just a pretentious affectation—or at least that, as affectations went, it was pretending to more than mere bonhomie. Adrian had felt slightly annoyed by it at first, but now he decided that it was acceptable, all things considered.

"I'm not thinking of it just as a stopgap or a stepping stone, Mr. Jarndyke," he assured the Yorkshireman. "My interest in your work is very serious, and I see it as a significant component of my own life's work."

"A component?" Jarndyke queried.

"My ambitions extend further than coloring textiles—but there's no reason why I can't pursue them all while operating from a base within your organization. I'm willing—eager, in fact—to make a long-term commitment. I'm not an orphan, but I'll be happy to broaden my family horizons."

"Broaden your family horizons?" Jarndyke repeated. "I'll remember that one. Okay, Son, you're a bright lad, so you know exactly why I'm interested in you and why I wanted to be the first in the queue to knock on your door, sixth months before you're officially scheduled to finish at Imperial. I've helped to bring about a revolution in the textile industry by growing fabrics from tissue cultures: first wools, then silks. In terms of texture, my products are already first-rate, and I've got top men working to make sure they stay that way. Thus far, though, I've remained reliant on the traditional dyeing industry for coloring my fabrics. Even if it hadn't been for the provocation of all the stupid media jokes about my supposed quest for the Golden Fleece, I'd have had to be blind not to see that genetically-determined pigmentation would be the natural next step in the process."

He tapped Adrian's CV, which was on the table in front of him, with the knuckle of his right forefinger. "I won't try to bullshit you, Son: according to this, and what my analysts tell me, on the basis of the engineering you've already done, you're absolutely the best man in the entire world right now to pick up that particular torch and run with it. For that reason alone, I'll hire you, but first, if only for the sake of settling my curiosity, tell me why a bright young reverse engineer like you—a genius, my experts say—would choose to specialize in a field like textile pigmentation, instead of joining the great crusade to save the planet from the ongoing ecocatastrophe, rid the world of disease and make us all immortal."

"You can see the results of coloration genes," Adrian said baldly, as he usually did when asked that question. "There's no waiting around while the DNA strings you've designed and the proteins they produce go through elaborate testing schemes administered by bureaucrats. Then again, the delicate sculpting of the relevant proteins, not merely to duplicate but also to enhance the extraordinarily elaborate palette of nature's colors, is a technical process that poses fundamental challenges of method and understanding. The fact that you can see the results immediately when working with

27

pigmentation genes, and thus connect up biochemi-
cal cause and effect directly, helps to provide a useful
insight into the mysterious workings of amino-acid
destiny, which is transferable to other areas where the
evidence is far less obvious. Mendel started off the
entire science of genetics by studying the heredity of
manifest characteristics like color, because it was the
most practical starting-point. It's still an important
gateway to genomic understanding."

"Gateway to genomic understanding?" Jarndyke
echoed, pensively. "You like the glib phrases, don't you?
Cut the bullshit, Son, and tell me the truth. You're
too bright to know that I wouldn't look behind this
thing"—he tapped the CV again—"because you know
as well as I do that what's really important is always
what's left out. The job offer stands, so you don't have
anything to worry about on that score. I just want to
know what you're about before you join the crew of
the Airedale *Argo*—and I want to hear it from you, as
straight as you can. With your qualifications and bud-
ding reputation, you could go anywhere you want, so
why do you want to work for me?"

Adrian swallowed his saliva and hesitated—not because he had not expected to have to come clean, but
because, in spite of what he had said to Artemus Clark
the day before with such airy self-confidence, he was
not entirely sure that Jason Jarndyke would be able and
willing to take aboard the more original and unusual
aspects of his argument. Ready or not, he wasn't used
to being hustled in the fashion that Jarndyke seemed
to find so natural. He was used to academic discus-

sions, which sometimes became waspish, but in which nothing was really at stake except pride and prejudice, and in which it was easier to set one's own pace and use glib phrases as stepping stones. As he had told his PhD supervisor, all that he had to do was tell his future employer the truth, and show him that, whether he believed them or not, following up his hypotheses was a risk worth taking, a venture worth trying.

"I do have my own personal reasons for being interested in the genetics of pigmentation," he admitted.

"Well, don't beat around the bush, Son—we don't do that up north. I already know what they are, because my spies are too good to leave anything out of their reports, but I really want to hear it from your mouth, because that's the only way I'm going to get a firm grip on them. So explain to me, please, in simple terms, why you think you can see more than other people can, and how you think that working for me is going to help you prove it to the doubting Thomases."

Adrian knew that he couldn't avoid a certain amount of beating around the bush, and he wanted to give the explanation at his own pace, so he decided to stick to the same spiel he had given Artemus Clark to begin with, unsure as yet of how much further he might be obliged or willing to go thereafter.

"Sight," he said, launching forth into the familiar argument, "is a three-phase process. People differ in all three respects. Phase one is what the retina can register; all eyes are slightly different. You doubtless remember the old schoolboy riddle about whether what you see as red is the same as what I see as red, even though we've both learned to *call* it red. Physiology tells us that it's a good question. Different people's retinas really do differ in their sensitivity to particular wavelengths of light and the neuronal signals they transmit in response."

"So?" Jarndyke prompted.

Adrian didn't want to be hurried; if he was going to give Jarndyke the explanation of his own special abilities, he wanted to make sure that the groundwork was in place. "The second phase," he said, "is the other end of the initial neuronal chain: what the cells of the brain pick up from the signals transmitted by the optic nerve and how they process it. Everybody's brain is slightly different; identical signals, if there are any, don't always produce the identical results in making raw information available to consciousness."

"Which is phase three," Jarndyke put in, to demonstrate that he was keeping up. "Different minds, different interpretations again. Some people are color blind. Some people have no taste—I'm one of them, according to Angie. This I know. So what? Not in terms of philosophical paradoxes, but in terms of material difference."

"People differ in their perception of color and sensitivity to its nuances," Adrian said, still refusing to be hurried, but now deliberately slanting the argument in the direction that might seem crucial to the industrialist, "but the number of people whose physiology makes them objectively incapable of discriminations—as in color blindness—is relatively small. Most insensitivity occurs at the level of consciousness. The individual's brain can discriminate, and does—but the mind sometimes takes no notice.

"Lots of people are unaware of color clashes when they dress, or when they look at other people's costumes—but the fact that they're consciously unaware doesn't mean that they're immune to the subtle effects of color that they're registering physiologically. It really does make a psychological difference what colors you put on your bedroom walls, whether you're consciously aware of it or not. You really can be driven mad by creepy wallpaper. And you might not know, when you look at someone else's outfit, what message it's sending to your brain—but that doesn't mean that it isn't making a difference to your perception of them, and hence to your attitudes and your treatment of them. Power-dressing works, especially if it's cleverly color-coordinated.

"Color matters, Mr. Jardyke, in textiles as in everything else. Esthetics matter. Some people might not know exactly how or why they matter, and they might even sneer at the people who can bring those things to the level of consciousness, but what we see and what we wear makes far more difference to our attitudes and responses than insensitive people are able to bring to the level of conscious thought."

Jarndyke was still waiting for him to get to the nub of the matter, perhaps impatiently, but he was now putting on a show of thinking hard, no longer trying to spur him on.

"Your business sense and the inventive acumen of your genetic engineers have made you the most successful textile manufacturer in the world, Mr. Jarndyke," Adrian coninued. "As you just said, in terms of efficiency of production and texture, your wools, silks and hybrids are near-perfect. In terms of the sense of touch, they're practically unbeatable, but in terms of the sense of sight—especially color—they have a long way to go."

"We're supposed to be talking about you, Son, not me," Jarndyke pointed out. "Personal reasons, you said, and that's what I've been told. You can see more colors than the rest of us, or think you can—isn't that the gist of it?"

"That's right," Adrian replied, gathering his courage. "Some people have perfect pitch—they can hear music more clearly and more subtly than their fellows, because they can discriminate the notes more precisely. Others can hear a wider range of sounds, are able to hear the sonic signals emitted by bats—and even sounds that aren't consciously apprehended can have an effect, if only in the crude sense of giving people headaches, or just a sense of unease. I have the visual equivalent of that kind of enhanced auditory sensibility. I have—or, as you put it, I think I have—better color sensation than the vast majority of people.

"My enhanced color sensibility is doubtless partly due to my retinas, and to the neural equipment of my brain too, but most importantly, I believe that I'm fully conscious of what they're registering, and that might be even rarer. Every body differs in that regard, of course, as many people having better than average color sensibility as have worse than average. I'm not claiming that there aren't people in the world even more sensitive than I am, but I do believe that I'm sufficiently better than average, and clever enough in applying my better sensibility, to do what you need me to do in improving your products, and more."

Jarndyke frowned slightly. "I've told you, Son," he said, "that you don't need the sales pitch. I know you can make me money, with or without being able to see twice as many colors as the man in the street. That's not what I'm asking you. What I want to know is how your mini-superpower links into your fondness for looking at paintings and your interest in psychology."

Adrian was slightly puzzled by that insistence, but he was not caught at a loss. "Well, obviously," he said, "I'm interested in trying to find out more about the ability I have—to understand its physiology and explore its potential. I'm interested in looking at paintings because I can see in the work of certain painters that they have an enhanced color sensitivity, like mine—and, perhaps even more interesting, in a general rather than a specific sense, evidence of different kinds of visual enhancement. It's trivially true, of course, that everyone who looks at a painting sees a different painting, partly because of their particular visual capacities, and partly because their different interests make them pay attention to different aspects of the image, but in my case, I think that I can sometimes see aspects of paintings to which other people are blind, which enable me to see a markedly different image.

"The interest in psychology follows from that, in several different ways. Given that the use of color and imagery in paintings evokes psychological responses in other spectators, I'm very interested in the way in which differences in color and imagery of which most people aren't consciously aware, but which are nevertheless really present, might affect them subliminally. If you like, I'm interested in unpacking the ancient cliché: 'I don't know anything about art, but I know what I like.' I'm interested in exploring the reasons why people are drawn to some color and imagery, and repelled by others—the esthetics of beauty and the esthetics of antipathy.

"I'm interested, too, in the psychology of painters who are incorporating elements into their work to which they know most people are blind. Are they simply addressing those aspects of their work purely to an elite minority, or are they actually trying to manipulate subliminal effects? It's probably an insoluble enigma, given that the painters themselves were probably not fully conscious of what they were doing, and why, but it fascinates me . . . and I hope that it doesn't make me seem less useful to you, because it's such a long way from your specific concerns. My hope is that working for you will give me an opportunity to follow up on my interests in esthetics and psychology, which I couldn't find in any other field of applied genetic engineering."

While he spoke, he became aware that Jason Jarndyke was looking at him with an odd intensity, as though he were harboring a suspicion that he didn't want to spell out, fishing for an item of information not yet contained in the explanations that he had so far solicited. For a man who supposedly didn't approve of beating around the bush, Jarndyke now seemed to be showing a surprising aptitude for that dubious art.

"I gather that you've had difficulty in the past convincing people that you really can see things they can't?" the industrialist said, tentatively.

Adrian nodded, resisting the temptation to loosen his tie. "Some people," he admitted, "think I'm . . . well, bullshitting, as you put it. Seeing is believing, they reckon, and if they can't see something, they can't believe in it. They refuse to believe that there are discriminations of color that they can't perceive themselves, even though they know that color-blindness is a familiar phenomenon."

Jarndyke nodded slowly. "But you've met other people who can make the same discriminations?" he said.

"To some degree," Adrian admitted. "I've run into others who are better than average, but I've never met anyone with my degree of sensitivity—not in the flesh. I know they exist, though, because I can see it in their works. Claude Monet, Dante Gabriel Rossetti and Caravaggio, to name but three. There are—or have been—hundreds."

"All painters."

"It's in painting that the evidence becomes clear, at least to me. They're not the only people who can reflect their enhanced perception in their work—fashion designers can surely do it too—but painters are the most obvious. There are doubtless thousands who don't produce any tangible evidence. I haven't produced any evidence myself, as yet—but I hope to do so."

"Why didn't you become a painter?"

That question surprised Adrian slightly, but he met it with a wry smile. "Because I can't draw," he said. "I can see, but I don't have the hand-eye coordination that would allow me to reproduce what I see. I can visualize shapes very well, even in three dimensions, but I can't reproduce them with my incompetent fingers and a pencil or a brush. I don't have the kind of design-control that would allow me to be an adept abstract expressionist, like Jackson Pollock. Sometimes, I think that I'm only half the person I might have been, with only half a talent, but I'm not entirely certain that even the great painters were a great deal more fortunate. After all, the number of people who can measure their true achievement—consciously, at any rate—is very small. Can I talk about textiles again now? I know I don't need the sales pitch, but I really would like you to understand where I might fit in with your enterprise."

Jarndyke frowned, and his mouth twisted into what might have been an expression of annoyance, but he nodded his shaggy head. "Go on," he said.

"In the beginning," Adrian said, "what I can do for you is help to produce a basic color range for your various fabrics. I'm a geneticist; I don't expect to be involved in the tailoring end of your operation. Because I'm interested in the psychology of color as well as its genetics, and the way that the two intersect and interact, I'd like to employ your fabrics to conduct research in that area, partly for my own esthetic satisfaction, but partly because the results of that research will surely have some practical application for you, in terms of making your fabrics, quite literally, more attractive.

"In the fullness of time, I hope that I might be able to help your designers understand what they need, in terms of coloring your fabrics for particular styles of tailoring. I won't be able to give you natural patterns for a while, yet—even stripes and polka-dots might take a decade or so—but when I can, I think I'll be able to work out the best color combinations. I hope that I can not only give you the best reds, the best blues, the best browns and the best blacks, but good combinations and designs—and good advice as to how to use them for maximum subliminal effect.

"I hope that you'll see the effect on your balance-sheet of my initial labors by the end of next year, but that might be only the beginning. With the opportunities you can give me . . . well, I really don't know as yet what might be possible, but I would like the chance to find out. There's a lifetime's work in it, and more, but I'm keen to make what progress I can. I can't draw, so I could never be a painter, but I can think, and I am a scientist, and I can hope to do what the painters never could: understand. I could do that sort of research in Academe, I suppose, but I really do think I'd have more incentives and more opportunities—and I'm not just talking about salary and equipment—working in your industry, Mr. Jarndyke. That's why I was so pleased to hear from you, and why I'm so grateful to your spies. That's not bullshit—it's the simple truth."

Jarndyke's eyes looked him up and down, and Adrian felt that every physical symptom of his youth and innocence was being interrogated, skeptically. He knew that he didn't really look the part, especially in the suit and tie that felt like fancy dress. He didn't *look* like an Argonaut of science, let alone the possessor of a mini-superpower. He knew full well that, in physical terms, he probably looked like a weakling, and delicate to boot—but every word he'd said really was true, and he hoped that he had said enough to make Jason Jarndyke doubt the evidence of his own unpolished eyes, and the blunt common sense that guided them.

"So," Jason Jarndyke said, eventually, "you're telling me that, given time, you can make me the *authentic* Golden Fleece?" He didn't smile ironically, as Artemus Clark would undoubtedly have done. "Not just golden, but magical."

"You could put it like that," Adrian conceded. "At least, I can try."

"Then I really don't have any alternative but to hire you, do I?" the businessman said, casually. "And not merely to hire you, but to let you go your own mysterious way once I have you securely ensconced in the *Argo*. That's fine. The job's yours right here and now, if you want, but you can have time to think it over if you want. I don't think anyone will beat my initial salary offer, but if they do, I'll match any offer you get from elsewhere, plus ten per cent. I'll take full responsibility for squaring you financially with Imperial, latent commercial potential-wise, and for transferring all your work in progress from London. Don't worry about breakages and disruptions—my removal men are the best in the business. And I'll play along with your personal agenda as best I can—you have my word on that. There are three conditions, though."

"No problem," Adrian assured him, but added, for form's sake: "What are they?"

"One: you have to move to headquarters, in Airedale, and you have to observe the security protocols in place there. I need you working in *my* lab, behind *my* security-wall, under *my* beady eye. I'll provide you with an apartment to begin with, and although you can get a place of your own if and when you want, it has to be local—no further away than Shipley. No telecommuting, no gallivanting, no loose talk. We live in an era of intense industrial espionage, and I'm in a highly competitive business, so I need to keep my people under wraps. Okay?"

"Fine," said Adrian.

"Two: you have to deliver on your promises. I don't like to be disappointed, and I really hate it if I find out that someone's been bullshitting me, because it hurts my pride to think that it might be possible for someone to take me for a ride. Once you sign on to work with me, you have to be part of the team and you have to deliver. Okay?"

"Absolutely."

Adrian had already nodded his head twice while replying, having expected nothing less, and he was poised to repeat the gesture, when, Jason Jardyke said, in exactly the same tone: "Three: you keep your hands off my wife."

Shocked to the core, Adrian blinked hard several times, and forgot to nod.

Then Jarndyke grinned, broadly, and said: "I knew I could throw you off your stride. Just winding you up, Son—except, of course, that if you were to violate that particular condition, I'd have to kill you. There are firing offences, and there are shooting offenses." He was still beaming, as if to make it obvious that it was a joke—a Yorkshire joke, orientated to a peculiar sense of humor, but a joke nevertheless—but it seemed to Adrian that there was something false about the smile, as if there were some secret behind it that Jason Jarndyke was nursing carefully.

Adrian suspected, strongly, that if the Yorkshireman had brought his wife into the discussion it wasn't simply to make a stupid joke, and he couldn't believe even for an instant that Jarndyke might think that he was capable of making an attempt to seduce his wife. Like him, Jarndyke had a hidden agenda—but Adrian had no idea what it might be. He didn't think it mattered, at least for the time being. He had the job, and that was the important thing. He didn't expect any significant problems to arise in respect of Jarndyke's apparent jealousy, even if Angelica Jarndyke turned out to be the kind of Medea that Dante Gabriel Rossetti might have invested with all kinds of alluring charms, including a few imperceptible to the common eye.

"I'm sure I can comply with all your requirements," Adrian said, all too conscious of how frail his voice might sound—but he'd never claimed to have perfect pitch, merely an ability to perceive a visual spectrum more complex than Isaac Newton had ever been able to dream of.

"Good," said Jarndyke, extending his meaty hand to be shaken. "We have a deal, Son. Enough of piddling billions—let's make me a *real* fortune."

3

Relocation from London to Jason Jarndyke's industrial estate, in the Aire valley between Bingley and Shipley, was easy enough and almost painless. As the industrialist had promised, he squared the financial arrangement with the university without any difficulty, and his removal men really were the best in the business. Under Adrian's careful supervision, they packed and unpacked all his essential equipment and his entire genomic library, while keeping the experiments in progress in perfect order. Within a matter of days, the private lab that he'd been assigned seemed like home—far more so, at any rate, than the well-equipped and well-designed apartment provided for him in a custom-built block within walking distance of what the locals called "the biotech building." That seemed to Adrian more reminiscent of a suite in the kind of hotel he'd never been able to afford to stay in. The fact that the building had a "concierge" and a staff of cleaners only added to the impression.

Adrian didn't really have anyone in London to whom to say goodbye except Professor Clark. Because he had invested so much time and effort in his work, only making room outside of that to feed his passion for art galleries, he had never even tried to form any significant amities, let alone amorous relationships. He had scores of nodding acquaintances, but no friends. Apart from his lab equipment and his web-connection devices, he did not even have much in the way of personal possessions. He had never been able to afford actually to buy works of art, any more than he had been able to afford to stay in fancy hotels, and he was all too well aware of the fact that prints only reproduced the aspects of painting that ordinary people could see, and never got the colors exactly right. He had never wanted to put that kind of ersatz art on his walls, or collect it in books.

He filled a trunk with clothes, but he had almost nothing of intimate significance to put on top. He was aware of how sad that might make him seem to an objective but color-insensitive eye, but he really didn't care. It wasn't his fault that he was an introvert, after all, and he didn't think that it was a *fault*, as such, in any case. Yes, he'd been married to his studies with an obsessive intensity, for seven long years, since turning eighteen and leaving school, but that had been required by his life-plan, which couldn't be similar to other people's life-plans, because he wasn't like other people—because he could really *see*, and they couldn't.

Anyway, he thought, *if you're going to be obsessed, you have to take it seriously, don't you? No half-measures.*

Getting settled into the new labs and the new flat, once his life had been transported there was inevitably a little difficult psychologically, because, like all obsessive people, Adrian was fond of routine, but he was proud of being a voluntary obsessive rather than a compulsive one, able to adapt to circumstance if necessary. So he committed himself to the process of adaptation with all reasonable determination. The difficulties he experienced didn't stem from such simple things as the flat having nasty wallpaper, or that the new people in the labs adjacent to his own being unfriendly—indeed, the wallpaper was a very tasteful icy shade of egg-shell blue with unobtrusive silver arabesques, and his new colleagues, including the hot-shots from various parts of south-east Asia, seemed to take a conscientious pride in living up to the local delusion that Yorkshire folk were famed for their hospitality. The problems that arose were in him, not the environment, and the purely psychological discomfort that descended upon him like a particular shade of indigo when his work and domestic routines needed retuning were just an autonomic neuronal reaction.

Because he was conscious of the problem, however, and knew that it was a problem, he knew there was no danger of the unease spiraling into clinical anxiety or depression. Such syndromes might afflict others, but not him. He was a scientist; he knew that he could cope, and take new circumstances aboard, given time.

In consequence, he immediately set about using his time methodically and effectively. He introduced himself to all his colleagues, and tried conscientiously to figure out how each of them fitted into the great genetic project of producing fabrics in sheets without such inconveniences as breeding lambs, feeding them, shearing them and then doing all the mysterious things to the bundled fleeces that had once been necessary to turn them into merino sweaters, coats and skirts. He even visited the factories, which were all lined up along the banks of the Aire, because water was their most crucial limiting factor, given the enduring superabundance of atmospheric carbon dioxide and the ease of producing artificial light with any spectral composition the doctor might care to order.

He allocated five hours a day to the intensive study of all the data hidden behind Jarndyke's security wall, and was duly amazed by its extent, its complexity, and its sheer beauty. Adrian could visualize three-dimensional organic molecules, and even though their colors were invisible in chemical diagrams and computer simulations, he was still sensitive to the esthetics of their topology. He knew—not thought, but *knew*—that DNA was the most beautiful molecule in existence, the standard by which all others had to be judged, just as he knew that there were seven shades of improvement on chlorophyll's green in the spectrum of its super-efficient artificial rivals, all of which were potentially available to human costumes as well as artificial fixation of sunlight, especially the ones that the unwittingly half-blind massive majority thought of simply as "black."

He was only able to allocate five hours a day to that essential work initially, however, because he had to save some for his own private endeavors and projects— although that had to go on the back-burner for the time being, because the formal part of his employment inevitably overflowed the fifty hours a week officially allocated to it. The start-up labor wasn't just a matter of setting up his molecule-modeling programs, integrating them into the existing software systems and establishing a practical pipeline by which cyberspatial planning could be turned into solid product; it also involved such essentially messy supplements as interviewing and selecting assistants capable of working under his direction, and building them into a team-within-a-team. Awesomely efficient and dedicated as he was, he couldn't do *everything* himself.

Adrian hated messy work; it was too time-consuming—and there were, after all, only a maximum of available twelve hours in each single working day, because he had to sleep for seven, having long since given up on trying to train himself to get by on four, and he needed a further five for eating, relaxation and esthetic sensation. Some politicians, he knew, got by on five hours sleep and no relaxation or esthetic sensation at all, but they were just imbeciles who did nothing *but* messy work—and badly, to boot—while he was a true scientist, and a true seer. He had to look after his brain. That meant treating it well in all respects, not just making sure that it got an adequate dose of all the right oils and minerals.

Jason Jarndyke welcomed him when he first arrived, but didn't keep looking over his shoulder thereafter—not obtrusively, at any rate. For the first few weeks, Adrian hardly caught a fleeting glimpse of his employer in the distance, but he knew that it was only a matter of time before he received his first Official Visit.

Inevitably, the moment came—but Jarndyke was obviously sufficiently familiar with the new routine that Adrian had set up to slide into one of its interstices, so as not to throw him off his stride.

"How's it going, Son?" the big man asked, having appeared in the lab while Adrian was caught in one of the necessary lacunae that developed when he was waiting for his equipment to produce information necessary to permit him to take the next step in his project.

"I'm slowly getting a grip, Mr. Jarndyke," Adrian assured him. "The experiments I transferred from London are in full swing, and I'm adding supplements as fast as I can. I think I might be ready to set up some actual production runs in a mock-up shed within a month. If they go well, I'll probably be able to bring you a proposal for industrial incorporation in . . . maybe another five weeks, but let's say six, to be on the safe side. Co-adaptation to your tissue-culture genomes shouldn't be a problem—your genomic designers have done an excellent job, fundamentally as well as phenotype-wise."

"Don't be in too much of a hurry, Son," Jarndyke advised him. "This is a marathon, not a sprint. I understand that these things take their own time. Rome wasn't built in a day—and the poor buggers couldn't make it last, even with the time they actually took. We're better than that, and we're not slapdash. We want product, but we don't want hitches. Settle down first. My spies tell me you're working way too hard, even for someone in the grip of initial enthusiasm."

"I don't think so," Adrian said.

"I know that—and you're one of those silly sods who won't ever be told; I know that too. I've got half a hundred of your type in the building already; you probably know who I mean by now. You really do need to get out more, socialize a little—get yourself a girl friend. This place might not be London, but it's not a bloody cemetery, socially speaking. Take advantage of what it has to offer."

"I've been to see the Hockneys at Salt's Mill," Adrian said, defensively, although he wasn't entirely sure why he needed to be defensive.

"Bully for you," said Jarndyke, with a sigh, like a man who was used to being deliberately misunderstood. "Okay, your own time's your own time. I don't really have any right to have an opinion about it, and I'd be an idiot if I started trying to turn my oddball geniuses into mediocre human beings. I can't help taking an interest in the psychological welfare of my precious employees, though, and I'm a great believer in the stabilizing influence of relationships. Given your interest in psychology, you ought to understand that. You really ought to get a girl-friend—don't let the bluntness of the local lasses put you off. At any rate, come to dinner on Sunday. Proper dinner—two o'clock. Spend the afternoon at the Old Manse. And don't even think of trying to say no."

Adrian hadn't been thinking of making any such attempt. Sunday afternoon was usually study time, but he prided himself on not being inflexible, on being able to adapt to circumstance. Taking obsession seriously was one thing, but being imprisoned by it was something else. Complying with the boss's requests wasn't really socializing, in any case: it was part of the job.

"Thanks very much," he said.

"You don't have to dress up," Jarndyke assured him. "Leave the suit and tie at home. We're very informal at the Manse. You'll enjoy yourself—I guarantee it. I've got the best cellar in England . . . in Yorkshire, anyway. Just turn up, enjoy the grub and the company—and for God's sake try to relax."

Adrian nodded.

Jarndyke turned away, having apparently reached the bottom line, business-wise, but then he turned back, pretending that something of no real relevance had just occurred to him, although Adrian suspected strongly that it was anything but a genuine afterthought.

"Have you ever seen the Rothko Chapel in Houston, Texas?" the industrialist asked. He seemed to have a real talent for the unexpected, when he applied himself.

Adrian blinked several times. "As a matter of fact, yes," he said. "I went to an applied genomics conference in Houston a couple of years ago, and made a special trip."

"I thought you might have done," Jarndyke said, obviously having taken note of the conference in Adrian's CV. "What did you think of it—the chapel, that is?"

"Magnificent," Adrian said. "Brilliant work. I'm not sure I appreciated the religious context, being an atheist, but the artwork itself . . . I couldn't help thinking of it as an anticipation of the esthetics of artificial photosynthetics—I find SAPs beautiful too, if skillfully applied, and I'm very interested in tracking their evolution."

Jarndyke nodded his head, as if he'd expected to hear exactly that answer, bizarre as it might have seemed to most laymen, delivered in exactly those terms. "Angie dragged me to see the chapel once," he said, thoughtfully. "To me, the panels looked like so many black rectangles. I just couldn't see what all the fuss was about. Emperor's new clothes, I thought. Nothing really there, but these arty types love to pretend, just to make suckers of the rest of us—not that I let on to Angie, obviously. I was wrong, was I?"

"Yes, Mr. Jarndyke," said Adrian, not beating about the bush. "They're not just black. There are other colors in there, if you have the eyes and mind to see them. They really are superb—but it's not your fault if you can't perceive the subtleties. It's your eyes, or your brain . . ."

"Or my stupid consciousness," Jarndyke concluded. "Don't have to sugar-coat it, Son. I know my limitations. Solid artificial photosynthetics just seem black to me as well, not to mention black panthers. But you can see the spots on the panthers, can you? And patterns evolving in SAP plaques?"

"I'm not all that unusual, in that respect," Adrian said, warily. "Lots of people can make out spots or stripes on the pelts of melanic animals, and it was only to be expected that artificial photosynthetic compounds would become subject to mutation and natural selection as soon as they were deployed, and that the results of that selection would modify their coloration, not necessarily randomly. You can probably see it yourself it in the indigos and purples, if you look hard. The blacks are more subtle, but it really is the case that there are shades of black, just as there are shades of red, yellow and blue—not all of them obvious to common eyesight—and shades of white too."

"But there's something particularly *disturbing* about variations of black, isn't there?" Jarndyke queried. "It's one thing to modify the tint of the silk and satin of eternal little black dress, but when it comes to seeing in the dark, and ominous shadows . . . well, that's something else, isn't it?"

Adrian was strongly tempted to tell his employer to stop beating round the bush, but judged that the time had not yet come. He reckoned that he needed to do a little more bush-beating himself, in order to figure out exactly why Jason Jarndyke was interested in shades of black and "ominous shadows." But not now; the natural pause in his endeavors was about to reach its end, and it was time for obsession to take over again.

"It's an interesting question," he replied, with the utmost neutrality.

"Yes it is," said Jason Jarndyke. "I might have more than one treat in store for you on Sunday. Might not, of course—how can I tell?—but something of interest, anyhow. I'd value your honest opinion, I really would." He stressed the word "honest" very slightly, but enough to serve as a warning. Adrian had no idea why such a warning might be necessary, or what "treats" the Old Manse might have in store for him, in addition to its cuisine and its wine-cellar.

Adrian wondered, briefly, whether Jarndyke might have bought a Rothko painting—or, at least, whether he was beginning to put together an art collection of some sort, as all billionaires seemed to feel obliged to do, whether they had any eye for art or not. Apparently, Angelica Jarndyke did have an eye for art, or thought she did, and probably wanted to guide her husband's purchases, as many billionaires' wives seemed to feel obliged to do.

"I look forward to it, sir," Adrian said, not entirely dishonestly.

"You can call me Jayjay, now," the industrialist said. "Once you've been invited to Sunday dinner, you're not just one of the family, but one with nickname status."

Adrian took note of a slight hint of anxiety about the latter part of that statement, but he was unable to formulate a hypothesis as to why his employer might be anxious about what was, after all, a routine visit, in accordance with a well-tried formula. Surely, the responsibility to make a good impression weighed entirely upon him, not the Jarndykes.

"See you Sunday, then," said the industrialist, casting an approving eye over the lab before making for the door.

Adrian contented himself with a grateful nod, not wishing to risk using his permission to use his employer's nickname as yet.

4

Adrian did not tell anyone that he had been invited to "dinner" at the "Old Manse" on Sunday afternoon, but Jarndyke's security walls were specifically designed to keep secrets from getting out of his laboratories, while permitting their free circulation within. That circulation was supposed to be on a need-to-know basis, but research scientists were notoriously liberal in their interpretation of what they needed to know. Everybody tended to drop in on everybody else's labs as and when they liked, on any pretext or none at all. It was part of the fundamental social dynamic of the place, which transcended barriers of nationality, and even scientific specialism. Everybody knew about the invitation in any case, because they knew that it was part of Jarndyke's routine, and it was hardly surprising that a small number wanted to offer him useful advice, as a gesture of morale-building team play.

"Don't worry about the obligatory expedition to Bleak House, Ade," said a Singaporean, who probably had not been called Chester Hu by his parents but had followed the common custom of adopting a Western forename for convenience, and who had decided off his own bat to call Adrian "Ade." "It's just a *rite de passage*, to welcome you to the extended family. Watch out for Medea, though."

That was a joke, of course, of the same silly ilk as the Dickensian reference, but because it was the second time that Adrian had heard the joke in question, and was a little worried about his ability to get through the *rite de passage* with flying colors, he paused to wonder whether there might something behind it, and whether Artemus Clark's joke had really been improvised out of mythological thin air rather than distant rumor.

"Why?" he asked.

"Oh, don't be scared. She won't try to seduce you, pale and pretty as you are. She's a dutiful trophy wife, faithful to her bargain, and she obviously likes masculine men as well as rich ones—but she's a little crazy, is all. People would probably have nicknamed her Medea anyway, given all the newsfeed jokes about Jason and the quest for the Golden Fleece, and given that Jayjay plays along with it with his Airedale *Argo* nonsense, but . . . well, I'm not at all sure that she doesn't think that she actually *is* a witch. Not gene-twisting witchcraft, of course—genuine mumbo-jumbo."

"She has no reason to put a spell on me," Adrian said colorlessly.

"Except that you're the hero who's actually promised to deliver the authentic Golden Fleece," Dr. Hu reminded him. "No—just joking. She's just a little weird, as I say. Don't let her put you off, if she's in one of her moods. She can be sulky, but she doesn't mean any harm. Jayjay's the one you have to impress—and you haven't put a foot wrong so far, Golden Boy."

"Weird how?" Adrian wanted to know, for safety's sake.

"She'll probably look at you in a funny way—and then, if she doesn't like what she sees, she won't look at you again. She doesn't like trivia, or dressing things up—she won't have knick-knacks on the mantelpieces, apparently, or paintings on the walls . . . not even prints. It's Bleak House up there, as I said. All plain wood paneling—brown by the acre, not a splash of color; more like a monastery than a house. You'll find it even duller than I did, I dare say, given your color sensibility. There must be other eccentricities, but those are the ones that will leap out at you. Don't worry about it. I'd say, turn a blind eye, but that's not really your thing, is it?" He smiled.

Adrian ignored the gibe. "What about Mr. Jarndyke's art collection?" he asked.

"He doesn't have an art collection," Hu informed him. "Maybe he wanted one—Angelica probably did—but if so, they shelved the project. Artistic disagreements, at a guess—real ones, not euphemistic. Angelica paints, so rumor has it—actually has a barn of sorts for her own private studio, that no one but her ever goes into, where she does whatever witchy stuff she does, but there are none of her paintings on the walls of the Hall. Not downstairs, at any rate. Maybe they're too pornographic to be allowed out of the bedroom."

Adrian was puzzled, sensing a mystery in the evolving pattern of information. Chester Hu didn't seem to think that there was anything to what he'd said but a report of arbitrary eccentricity, but Adrian wasn't at all sure, now that he could put what Jason Jarndyke had said to him into a different informational context. The weird and moody Angelica Jarndyke had "dragged" her husband to see the Rothko chapel, but wouldn't tolerate paintings on the walls of their home . . . not in the spaces that visitors saw, at any rate. She was "rumored" to be a painter herself, but the likes of Chester Hu had never seen any of her work. No one was allowed in her "studio," but Jason Jarndyke had "more than one treat" for him after Sunday dinner—or maybe not. Something that might interest him, at any rate.

"Don't look so worried," Chester said. "It really isn't that bad. Just go along with it. Do you know who else he's invited?"

Adrian blinked. "I didn't know he'd invited anyone else," he said.

"It figures," the Singaporean said. "Didn't he give you the spiel about the stabilizing effect of relationships and advise you to get a girl-friend?"

"He did mention something like that. I didn't take any notice."

"He takes it seriously, and he also fancies himself as a matchmaker. He always rounds out the numbers when he invites one of us up to the Manse. He'll have invited some youngish woman from Shipley—not an employee, because he thinks in-house sexual relationships are incestuous—ostensibly just to make up a full table, but really to give you a nudge in the dating direction . . . and perhaps to deflect some of your attention away from darling Angelica. After all, he doesn't want to risk his employees falling hopelessly in love with her and being distracted from their work in that direction, does he?"

Perhaps, Adrian thought, Professor Clark's Medea joke hadn't simply been a matter of mythological free association after all. Perhaps he had heard a rumor of some kind. And perhaps Jason Jarndyke's third condition hadn't simply been a random shot aimed in jest to shake his complacency and make him blink.

He was almost tempted to ring Professor Clark to ask him exactly what he had intended to imply, but couldn't face the thought. He wondered whether he ought to look up the legend of the Golden Fleece in more detail, because he remembered something in that connection, very vaguely, about dragon's teeth, and was fairly certain that Medea had been one of the original *femmes fatales*. He knew that anything he extracted from a web search about the nature and scope of the legendary Medea's sorcery would be just so much bullshit, but there was no harm in taking a look. Not that it mattered even if Angelica Jarndyke actually did fit that sort of stereotype. This was the twenty-first century, after all, and the only magic abroad in the world was that inherent in applied genomics, high-temperature conductivity, coincidence theory and controlled sub-atomics. A genius of his sort, or any other, could not possibly have any fear of mere traditional witchcraft.

He did, however, take the precaution of asking a couple of his other male colleagues about what he might expect in the course of the Sunday dinner *rite de passage* that they had undergone in their turn.

Both of them agreed with Chester Hu.

"It's no big deal," said Martin Rutledge, one of the few other Englishmen on the biogeek team. "Jarndyke's heart is in the right place. He won't be offended if nothing comes of his attempt to fix you up. To tell the truth, I don't think he expects it to. To some extent, he's just adding a little extra protection in case Angelica is in one of her downbeat moods. Don't get me wrong— she's a lovely woman, and always makes every effort to be polite and pleasant, but it's well-known that she's prone to fits of deep depression. She's sometimes very obviously on edge, and sometimes taciturn. She does her best, poor thing, but sometimes she can't quite rise to the occasion. If that's the case on Sunday, just cut her a little slack. Jayjay can talk for two, obviously, but he's learned from experience that it always helps to have an extra mouth at the table, in more ways than one. And he's not a bad judge of compatibility—he'll make sure that any girl he invites will have the right fodder for conversation. You like art, which will make it easy for him—and easier for Angelica too, I guess. You've been to the gallery in Salt's Mill, I suppose?"

"Yes."

"You like Hockney?"

"Yes, very much. An excellent eye for color and subtle seasonal transformations, and always enterprising in his technique."

"Well then, there won't be any problem. Plenty of diehard Hockney enthusiasts in these parts. You could do worse than let the old man fix you up, if he can. He's always over the moon if one of his matchmaking ventures actually manages to make a match, and they sometimes do. I didn't hit it off with the girl he laid on for me, but that wasn't his fault."

"Have you ever seen any of Angelica's paintings?" Adrian asked, curiously.

"No—but I don't think they're actually secret. She might just be embarrassed about showing them, even though she studied at the Courtauld way back when, and can't be completely devoid of talent and technique. Given your interest, and the fact that he'll try to find someone with similar interests to make up the foursome, you might well get to see some. Ask, if you're interested—can't hurt. Even if she only paints as therapy, to counter her depression, she must take a certain pride in her work."

Adrian remembered what Jason Jarndyke had said about perhaps having more than one treat in store for him, in a context that suggested strongly that he was not only thinking about painting but about paintings in which he, personally, could not see something that was supposed to be there, perhaps in shades of black.

Adrian remembered the hidden agenda that he had suspected during his interview, and was strongly tempted to take the inference that Angelica Jarndyke, like him, was possessed of a degree of enhanced color sensibility, perhaps even to a similar extent.

If so . . .

But it was too soon to start tracking the implications of that hypothesis. First, it needed to be put to the proof. If he could measure her powers of discrimination through her painting, then Sunday dinner might be, if

not exactly a "treat," at least an interesting revelation—
and a topic of conversation of a kind that he had never
had an opportunity to develop before.

An Austrian born and brought up in Vienna, and
obviously respectful of his own local traditions, Horst
Koerner, took a more earnest and academic approach
to the business of giving advice.

"What you have to remember, Adrian," he said, "is
that Mr. Jarndyke exhibits all the symptoms of a classic
inferiority complex: a stubborn drive to succeed in all
respects in life, which conceals a deep-seated anxiety
that he might fail. That helps to make him the bold
and innovative businessman that he is, and drives his
attitude to his trophy wife, of whom he is both exceedingly proud and exceedingly possessive. You must
admire her, but not lasciviously or flirtatiously. That
should not be difficult; she is a very beautiful woman,
although her looks are beginning to fade now that she
is past forty, but she is cold and not at all flirtatious.
She probably does not love him, but she is very glad of
the protection that he provides for her own frailty and
innate anxiety, and knows how precious it is that he is
besotted with her. Be respectful and careful, and you
won't risk putting a foot wrong.

"In any case, if you want to ingratiate yourself, tell
Mr. Jarndyke that you detect the true spirit of Richard
Arkwright in his intelligence and his endeavor. He loves
that. And remember that you are one of the things of
which he is proud, an emblem of his acumen and enterprise. Try not to be too modest, if you can, but do
try to encourage the belief that you owe him a great

debt, and would not be able to achieve your ambitions without his support and patronage. That is the kind of flattery on which you ought to concentrate."

"Thanks," said Adrian. "That's very useful. Angelica, I presume, doesn't have an inferiority complex?"

"Indeed not. Rather than being driven to succeed, she seems to be something of a chronic underachiever. She is known to be subject to fits of clinical depression as well as anxiety, but never, so far as I know, to mania, so I would be very surprised if she were bipolar. I have not seen nearly enough of her to attempt a thorough analysis, but I suspect that hers is not the kind of depression that Prozac can address. Do you know Robert Burton's *Anatomy of Melancholy*?"

"I'm afraid not."

"You should—a fascinating text, one of the finest ever to come out of England, exceedingly rich in psychoanalytical interest. Having undertaken an exhaustive and almost Germanically rigorous analysis of various kinds of melancholy, in the hope of obtaining a better understanding of his own, he concludes that beyond all the environmental causes of temporary, and what one might call rational, melancholy, there is a deep-seated variety that is inexplicable in terms of external causes: a kind of resident self-dissatisfaction. One of your other philosophers, I believe, termed it 'Byronic unhappiness.' Many people afflicted with it turn, as Burton himself did, to obsessive writing or painting, often of an imaginative stripe, not so much as a means of escape, in my opinion, but as a kind of justificatory elaboration. If I could see Mrs. Jarndyke's paintings, I would have a clearer idea, but I have not been so fortunate. If she shows them to you—as she might well, given your artistic interests—I would be very interested to hear your impression of them."

"I hope I will. You don't think that she deserves her reputation as a witch, though?"

"Absolutely not. It is based on a ridiculous misconception, a side-effect of the careless fashion in which people sometimes refer to her as Medea—people who have never read Euripides, of course, and have probably never heard of him. I am a good enough judge of men, I think, to know that whether she qualifies as a trophy wife or not, Mr. Jarndyke would never dream of discarding her for a younger model, and I am perfectly convinced that if he did, she certainly would not murder her children as a reprisal. Indeed, I think Euripides was unjustified in that invention, which does not feature in earlier versions of the myth, and represents idle pandering to contemporary prejudices against women. When Dr. Hu insists on referring to the Jarndyke residence as Bleak House, that is merely silly, but calling Mrs. Jarndyke 'Medea' is blatantly offensive. Such careless wordplay would never be tolerated in Vienna."

"No doubt. Have you ever considered going into psychoanalysis yourself?"

"Indeed not. Armchair philosophy of any kind is best practiced as a hobby. If one wants to be happy, one must deal with the material, and its foundation. I am very glad and very proud to be a geneticist, and particularly glad to be working in the field of textiles. 'Clothes maketh the man,' as another of your great philosophers once said, and it is truer than he knew. The other primary biotechnology, cooking, tends to get more credit nowadays for its prehistoric contribution to the growth and sophistication of the intelligent brain, but the contribution made by clothing and its inorganic technological corollaries: sewing, spinning and so on, should not be underestimated. We are what we wear as well as what we eat, and the work that you and I are doing, my friend, is literally world-changing. Psychoanalysis is merely skimming the surface of identity, an aspect of the froth of technological determinism."

Adrian liked Horst; he appreciated his determined intellectual unorthodoxy and the broad range of the Austrian's interests. He promised himself that one day, he would ask him for his impressions of his own psychological make-up—but not yet, and perhaps not for a long time.

5

Jason Jarndyke's "Old Manse" was neither old, nor a manse. Not literally, at any rate. Horst Koerner, who had naturally researched the matter, had informed Adrian that it had been completed less than ten years before, having been seven years in the construction, to a design that Jarndyke had imposed on his reluctant architects by sheer will-power and bribery. Unkind people had called it a Folly, Horst had said, but unkind people with no respect for words always said things like that, and even if it had been a Folly, that didn't necessarily mean that it was unesthetic. Adrian knew that there could be grandeur in Folly, and even magnificence, even when there was an abundance of mere folly.

In fact, he rather liked the look of the house on top of the moor, although architecture wasn't really "his thing," as Chester Hu might have put it, and fake Portland Stone from northern France definitely wasn't his color. He preferred the honest blacks of the old stone walls on the moors and the old stone buildings in Shipley and Bingley, and he thought it a pity that they were gradually being swept away by decrepitude and demolition, and replaced with paler imitations. The Old Manse was an honest fake, not trying to be anything else. Adrian liked it, as seen from distance, and he still liked it at close range, as seen from the driveway, up which he walked because he had never owned a car and didn't want to face the embarrassment of having to ask some flunkey where he could put his bicycle. From the outside, the house wasn't bleak in his eyes.

Even though architecture wasn't really his thing, one of Adrian's carefully-planned esthetic excursions, while he had been at an AG conference in Derby, had been to see the site on the Derwent where the nineteenth-century industrialist Richard Arkwright had begun the first revolution of the textile industry, introducing automated machinery into his water-mills, and then replacing water-power with steam engines. The factories had been partially restored as a museum, and the house—the original version of which had been burned down—had served time as a hotel before being fully converted into a museum, but the ghost of Arkwright's intention had still been visible.

As the richest man in the north of England, and the effective kingpin of the *nouveau riche* of the First Industrial Revolution, Arkwright had wanted a palace from which an emperor might look down on his domain, and the source of his own magnificence—a modern palace, of course, not a mere copy of some Roman ruin or some scaled-down Versailles, but a palace nevertheless. Jason Jarndyke's Old Manse was by no means as pretentious as Arkwright's Victorian colossus, but that was a symptom of marching time and late twenty-first century notions of propriety: its stone walls and steeply-pitched slate roofs embodied, in essence, the same dream of domination and imperial justice. It did not symbolize vulgar wealth, or even brute power—Jarndyke wasn't as unsubtle as that—but it did constitute a testament of *merit*, of due desserts duly enjoyed.

Adrian could appreciate that, and approve of it; he was not one of the clichéd scientific geniuses who affected to despise men who "make money out of the inventions of others," because he knew how unusual the talent was that such triumphs required—and he knew that Jason Jarndyke, although certainly not free of egomania, thanks to what Horst Koerner had diagnosed as his incipient inferiority complex, had his vanity under strict control.

Inside, there were, as Chester Hu had put it, "acres of brown." Adrian didn't mind that, either, although it did seem a trifle austere, and he could understand why some people might find it bleak. Personally, he liked wood, especially old wood, with its swirling grain and knots. Whoever had cut and organized the paneling might not have had perfect sight, but Adrian quickly took note of evidence that might well have had slightly enhanced vision, and might have been ironically aware of it. Either way, he hadn't been a mug or a skimper.

Anyway, Adrian thought, *better austere and natural than contrived and awful*. He remembered what Chester had said, *en passant*, about Mr. and Mrs. Jarndyke probably having agreed to disagree about matters of decoration, and deciding on minimalism as the best compromise. Adrian got the same impression. They had probably wanted different things, and had decided on neither. He could approve of that, too.

It was also obvious why Drs. Hu and Koerner had been in rare agreement in describing Angelica Jarndyke as a "trophy wife." In terms of superficial appearance, she was almost a cliché: fifteen or twenty years younger than her husband, and radiantly beautiful, even now that she was past forty—so beautiful, in fact, as to be out of anyone's league but a millionaire's, at least—and carefully polished to boot, to the extent of seeming an item of artifice, more showpiece than person. Her dress sense was perfect, even though she was displaying "casual," and Adrian perceived at first glance that she was an expert in applying make-up; he had never seen artifice so flawless—but he had had a sheltered upbringing in that regard, and he knew it. She was tall—only an inch shorter than her husband, and five inches taller than Adrian—but her proportions were still perfect even at forty-something, and she still moved with consummate grace

Angelica Jarndyke was the first trophy wife that Adrian had ever encountered in the flesh, and he knew that all the ones he'd seen in photographs had probably been airbrushed, so he was slightly surprised to find that she wouldn't have needed airbrushing. If he didn't find her overwhelmingly attractive, it was partly because he found her height intimidating and partly because he had trained himself, for reasons of self-defense, not to find any woman attractive, in herself. One of the advantages of enhanced color sensation, he believed, was that a supersensitivity to color allowed him to look beyond the crude kinds of visual cues that stimulated inconvenient hormonal surges. The kind of beauty that formulated *his* truth was not the coarse beauty of common-or-garden lust. At least, he liked to think so.

When he was formally introduced to Angelica, Adrian, not knowing what to do, contented himself with a stiff and awkward bow. She looked him up and down, with just a little too much attention. Adrian had not expected that she would simply give him the once over and think: *Just one more mad scientist for Jayjay's collection*, and that did not seem to be what she was thinking at all. Unfortunately, Adrian couldn't read what the thinking actually was that lay behind in her particular lack of indifference, so it made him feel slightly anxious. Obviously, Jason Jarndyke had told her that the latest recruit to his team of geniuses had an extended sensibility to color variation, which would undoubtedly have piqued her interest if she had one too, but it obviously hadn't made her want to throw her arms open and greet him as a brother. If anything, she seemed suspicious and guarded, perhaps skeptical. He couldn't blame her for that; he was more than a trifle guarded himself, even more so on the present occasion than usual.

Whatever the case, and somewhat to his relief, given his anxiety, once Angelica Jarndyke had subjected him to a long and sharp inspection, she went on to do exactly what Chester Hu had predicted, looked away, and did not look directly at him again for some time. She did not give the impression of being deeply depressed at present, but anxiety was clearly lurking just beneath her polished artificial surface.

The other guest was also exactly what Chester Hu had predicted: a young woman from Shipley, seemingly slightly older than Adrian, but almost as slim and an inch shorter, who had recently been taken on as an assistant curator of exhibitions at the Salt's Mill gallery. Her name was Meryl Ingram. Like him, she was a southerner, from Bracknell in Berkshire, and had not been in Yorkshire long enough to have become culturally acclimatized. Although not beautiful in the sense that Angelica Jarndyke was, she was neat and composed, with wire-rimmed spectacles that had slight difficulty perching on her nose, the bridge of which was not very pronounced. She was simply dressed in pastel shades, but gave evidence of a certain admirable delicacy in her color sensibility. Adrian found her likeable, and precisely for that reason she provoked a certain studied reserve in his conversation, which seemed to find a counterpart in hers, although he was not at all confident that it was generated in the same way.

Adrian assumed that Meryl must have deduced that she had been invited to the meal in order to provide a partner of sorts for him, even if she was unaware of Jason Jarndyke's reputation for awkward matchmaking. He guessed that she was almost as embarrassed by that as he was, and equally determined to maintain a careful politeness that maintained a safe distance between them. He had no idea what would constitute an ideal match for him, if such a thing existed, but he was dubious that Meryl Ingram could qualify, for which he felt a certain perverse relief. That, at least, was one anxiety he could shelve.

The meal was excellent, although Adrian could not help feeling some discomfort because of the fact that it was served by two rather formal waiters, who, while stopping short of aping a TV butler in some historical drama, nevertheless seemed a trifle supercilious. The cuisine was basic, but top quality. Adrian had never tasted a Yorkshire pudding that had not come out of a freezer-bag, and he had to admit that there was a reward in authenticity, in that case as in so many others. The beef was tissue-cultured, of course—there was no point in taking "authenticity" to absurd lengths—but it was first rate, and Adrian would have been willing to bet that it came from cells descended from a local breed, not stereotyped Aberdeen Angus. He was no wine expert, but he couldn't find any fault with Jarndyke's much-vaunted cellar.

There were only the four of them at the table. Adrian knew that the Jarndykes had two children, both boys, but there was no evidence of their presence in the house, and Adrian assumed that they must both be away at a fancy prep school, being groomed for Oundle, or even for Eton. Meryl Ingram seemed to share his discomfort with regard to the servants to begin with, and because Angelica Jarndyke was also a trifle reticent at first, while Adrian was too shy to do anything much beyond reacting to what was said to him, Jason Jarndyke had to guide the initial chatter and do most of the talking himself, but he was obviously used to that and did it well.

The industrialist talked and talked throughout the first two courses, but he avoided being boring with practiced ease. He did not come across a boor, nor as overly arrogant, in spite of his cultivated bluntness and natural ebullience. He discussed current events and future possibilities—in a general sense rather than a specific one—with equal ease, and reminisced blithely without any crass braggadocio. Eventually, he succeeded in stimulating more detailed and relaxed contributions from his guests, as they gradually felt more at ease, and the conversation became even more amiable over dessert, when Angelica began to join in more artfully, provoking longer speeches with questions regarding Adrian's and Meryl's impressions of Airedale and explorations of their common interests, beginning with their appreciation of Hockney and progressing to mild criticism of the conspicuous obsolescence of the modernism of the Tate Modern, and the awful error that had been made in sandblasting York Minster and the Angel of the North.

Apparently motivated almost automatically by genuine sympathy, Angelica Jarndyke's interest seemed to warm up further when Adrian expressed enthusiasm for some of the lesser-known British painters of the nineteenth century, citing a particular admiration for John Martin and Richard Dadd.

"I know Martin's work," Jason Jarndyke put in, "but not Dadd's. Didn't he murder his father, though?"

"Dadd did murder his father during a psychotic break," Angelica said, "but that doesn't make him any less of an artist. Nowadays, he'd be diagnosed as a paranoid schizophrenic. There was madness in John Martin's family too—his brother, who was a clergyman, became known as Mad Martin after he tried to set fire to York Minster—long before the sandblasters ruined it. It's irrelevant to his brother's gifts as a painter. What do you like about their work in particular, Adrian?"

"To me, the most interesting thing about Dadd's art is his meticulous attention to detail, especially in the *Sketches to Illustrate the Passions*. He had a unique way of seeing, not vague and numinous like Turner's, but scrupulous and intense. You can see something of the same attentiveness in the tiny figures in Martin's earlier paintings, especially *Belshazzar's Feast*—although that had to be restored after being damaged, so it's difficult to evaluate it accurately."

"Did you see the recent exhibition of his work at the Laing in Newcastle, celebrating the fiftieth anniversary of the 2011 exhibition?" Meryl asked.

"Yes," Adrian confirmed, "I was able to make the trip. Were you involved with that?"

"Not professionally, but I went to see it."

"I took Angelica," Jarndyke put in, proudly. "I was very impressed—especially by his work as an inventor and a civil engineer. I admire versatility in genius. I'm no artist myself, alas, but I admire men who can spread themselves, and aren't just specialists—like yourself, Adrian. People think of businessman as utilitarians, in the bad sense of the word, but you can't be a narrow utilitarian in the textile business, where esthetics is fundamental, in both tactile and visual terms. I'd like to get Salt's Mill to put on an exhibition of Yorkshire textiles, old and new—I fear, Meryl, that that's my hidden agenda in inviting you here. I'd like you to discuss the proposal with you. If I can convince you that it's a good idea, perhaps you can organize it."

The suggestion seemed to renew the assistant curator's embarrassment, and Angelica was quick to step in again. "Well, I had no hidden agenda," she said. "I simply think the work you do is fascinating and valuable, Meryl, gathering material here from all over Europe, organizing it into a meaningful ensemble, drawing out and elaborating its themes."

"I'm only an assistant," Meryl observed. "I just do the grunt work. I'm not really involved in the planning. I don't have the seniority, and my publications record is too thin. You have to work hard to demonstrate your expertise nowadays to advance in the curating business, and I fear that I've been a trifle lax."

"You're still young," said Angelica. "It's just a matter of serving your apprenticeship. Your day will come, I'm sure."

Adrian noticed that Meryl seemed slightly nettled by the assertion that she was still young, although he could not believe that she was over thirty. She did not seem convinced that "her day would come." Indeed, he read what he thought was envy in a rapid glance that she cast at him, probably thinking that he, who was manifestly younger than she was, was already enjoying the glorious sunshine of his day.

Jason Jarndyke had either failed to notice the glance or misread its import. "You and Adrian are the future, Meryl," he said, in support of his wife. "I'm an old man now, past my peak and on the way down, but as long as I can nurture young genius like Adrian's—and yours if you'll agree to handle my exhibition project—I'm still making my contribution . . . and money, thank God."

There was a slight pause while coffee and brandy were served, and then the servants finally withdrew permanently, somewhat to Adrian's relief

Meryl turned to Adrian. "Are you really trying to engineer a golden fleece, as the newssites say?" she asked, trying to make the question seem flippant but seemingly genuinely interested.

"Certainly," said Adrian. "Both literally and meta-phorically. At present, the wool produced by tissue-culture follicles, either in fiber or planar form, is gray, and has to be dyed. My job is to introduce genes into the complex that will add pigments—not just gold, but all the colors in the rainbow, and more. Mother Nature has the ability not merely to produce all the colors we can see and a few that many people can't, but she can produce them in patterns as intricate as those of a butterfly's wing. My first task is to produce uniform colors of a particular richness and allure, and that will be no mean feat, but it's a beginning rather than an end. If the genes of a peacock butterfly—or, indeed, the bird after which it's named—can do what they do purely as a result of natural selection, there's no reason, theoretically, why an artificial gene-complex shouldn't ultimately be able to produce sheets of silks with in-built patterns even more complicated and beautiful . . . and perhaps, ultimately, as meticulously organized as a painting by Martin or Dadd."

"You really think you can do that?" asked Meryl, in an awestruck tone that was obviously synthetic.

"Probably not me, but those who come after me, hopefully building on groundwork I've laid."

"But it's not just a technical problem," Jason Jarndyke insisted. "Adrian has good eyes as well as clever hands. He can discriminate colors that other people can't, and he's learning how to manipulate psychological responses to colors, individually and in combination, that operate subliminally."

"Is it really true that you can discriminate colors that other people can't, Adrian?" asked Angelica, her stance relaxed and her tone light, but with a sudden intensity in her gaze. It was a prompt rather than a question, because Angelica knew the answer already, but he presumed that Meryl hadn't been briefed, and knew that he ought to make some effort to maintain her inclusion in the conversation.

"Yes, I can," he said, mildly. "I can't claim any credit for it—it's Mother Nature's gift—but I can see subtle shades of color that most people can't discriminate. It's not unusual in nature for the retinas of animals to discriminate visual spectra slightly more or less extensive than the human, probably classifying the colors they see in ways that are different from the five colors of the Newtonian spectrum, so it's not really surprising that humans differ slightly from one another in their color perception."

"Aren't there seven colors in the spectrum?" Meryl asked.

"According to Newton, yes. Perhaps he had better discrimination than most people, although it's more probable that he just wanted to make the number up to seven because he thought it had a special propriety. Modern color theorists tend to eliminate orange and indigo as fringe effects rather than separate colors—but that illustrates my point. To some people, at least, indigo seems to be more than simply a meeting of blue and violet, and orange also seems distinct from the overlap of red and yellow. Conventional classification of pigments also extents to include browns"—he waved a slender hand at the paneling on the dining room—"and grays, whose discrimination seems to indicate that black shouldn't be regarded as simply an absence of white. Some people, of course, can only see the world in shades of gray, and others can't discriminate red from green. What I can do isn't really that unusual—it doesn't set me apart from other humans, any more than being uncommonly tall or having a good ear for music."

"Adrian's just being modest," Jason Jarndyke put in, addressing Meryl. "At least, I hope he is, because I haven't hired him just to be a *little bit* different—I need him to be truly exceptional."

Adrian felt a little foolish, but he didn't want to seem boastful, and didn't quite know how to react to that. "Very few people have eyes that are free from myopia, presbyopia or any of the other physical flaws that can diminish sight," he said. "I'm just fortunate in seeming to be free of imperfections that afflict almost everyone to some degree, but it's difficult to make comparisons, especially because there seem to be other special ways of seeing, quite different from color sensitivity, of which less well-equipped individuals can pick up hints in artistic representations, like those of Martin and Dadd."

"That's interesting," Meryl commented, "and it's relevant to the kind of work I do. It's something of a cliché, obviously, that no two people see exactly the same painting, and that different artists see the world in different ways, so that they often put things into their work that onlookers may not see, but I hadn't thought of it in the terms you're using. Have you published anything on this?"

"Not in reputable scientific journals. There are a few essays in fringe publications—you can find most of them easily enough with a search engine, although my name inevitably gets confused with other Adrian Stamfords, so you need to add 'color' or 'esthetics' to the search criteria to help filter out the irrelevant material."

"I'll look them up," Meryl said.

Adrian didn't take the promise seriously, but he noticed that Jason Jarndyke seemed pleased, perhaps because it seemed to be forging a link between the two guests that he had brought together with that purpose in mind. The flash of satisfaction was almost immediately compromised, however, by a slight hint of impatience. Matchmaking was not the only item on his hidden agenda.

"If I can persuade Salt's Mill to put on a textile exhibition," he said, "Adrian will obviously play a significant role too—although I'll have to be careful not to overload him with responsibilities. I like my employees to be able to strike a healthy balance between work and leisure. I don't want my geniuses burning out. The quest is a marathon, not a sprint."

Again, Adrian did not know how to react to that, thinking that any kind of protest might give a wrong impression.

"There's no such thing as working too hard, Jayjay, as you well know," Angelica put in. "You really ought to let your employees organize their own lives in their own way."

"Of course," Jarndyke agreed. "You're right, as always. I worry too much. But if the future of my business depends on geniuses, then I do have to make what effort I can to preserve and maintain their genius, and provide it with an environment that will help it flower. I know how lucky I am that genetic scientists of the ability of Adrian, Chester Hu and Horst Koerner are prepared to work for me, in a relatively unglamorous industry, and I want them to be as happy as possible. That's just sensible economics."

"Fair enough, darling." Angelica conceded, "and from the little I see of your various protégés, you seem to be succeeding. But as Adrian says, people are different in all sorts of ways, and happiness isn't a one-size-fits-all sort of thing." Her gaze suddenly switched back to Adrian. "I admit to being a little surprised that you were so keen to accept my husband's offer of employment," she said. "I'm pleased, naturally . . . but I must confess to finding it a little odd. I'd have thought that someone with your ability would have been drawn in a different direction . . . into Meryl's world."

Adrian shrugged his shoulders, defensively. "Sight is just sight," he said. "To make something of it, it has to be combined with other skills, mental and physical. I'm a geneticist, so my unusual sight inevitably directed me toward the genetics of pigmentation, and I was fortunate enough to finish my PhD at the precise moment when a golden opportunity opened up for the practical employment of that knowledge. If I'd had different skills, then I suppose I might have been tempted to become a painter, but I think I might have found it very frustrating to be producing paintings in the knowledge that most people wouldn't be able to see the full effect that I was representing—as you're presumably well aware, Mrs. Jarndyke."

He had been following the thread of his argument, and had added the last remark almost without thinking. He realized a fraction too late that it might not have been diplomatic, given that Jason Jarndyke had refrained, perhaps carefully, from telling him explicitly that his wife had similar perceptive abilities to his. Angelica Jarndyke reacted as if she had had suffered a slight electric shock, and she shot an accusative glance at her husband.

"I didn't tell him, Angie," Jarndyke protested, "but he might have inferred it from the questions I asked. He is a genius, after all."

"I'm sorry," Adrian blurted out, almost simultaneously. "I didn't realize . . ."

But Angelica had already recovered her composure, and was quick to interrupt them both. "Of course," she said. "Jason hired you for that ability, after all. He could hardly help making the connection with me, and probing, in his customary unsubtle fashion, and of course you took the correct inference. It's just that, for a long time, it's been something of a touchy subject . . . for reasons of which, to borrow your own phrase, you're presumably well aware."

Her gaze had now become so intense that Adrian had the sensation of a knife passing through him. There was little or no sympathy in that gaze, and he found that disconcerting. He realized, however, that he was, indeed, very well aware of why it was "a touchy subject," which Angelica Jarndyke did not like to discuss, and why she was disappointed that her husband, however innocently and indirectly, had let the cat out of the bag. Like him, she must have had difficulty persuading others that her ability was real, and not an affectation or a delusion, and she seemed to have a much thinner skin than him. Her anxieties and tendency to depression were evidently connected to her additional sensitivity—and Adrian could not help drawing the inference, now, that her enhanced sensibility might not be slight, like that of a Monet or a Caravaggio, but extreme, like his own.

If so, Adrian thought, he might have made a mistake in understating the extent of his difference from the norm in conversation. If she were not only able to distinguish subtle shades of color, but able to see the elusive shadows too, that would be another matter entirely, and might be a matter of great relevance for both of them.

But she doesn't even want to believe that I really have enhanced color sensibility, Adrian thought, with certain puzzlement. *Even though she has it herself, she doesn't want to believe that I have it too! Why not? On the other hand, how can I blame her, when it's been so hard for me to believe all the revelations of my supersight myself? If she really can see the elusive shadows, it makes perfect sense that she'd be frightened . . . She must be ambivalent about the possibility of finally being proved sane. Who can blame her? Not me, for sure.*

The person who did not understand what was going on at all, of course, was Meryl Ingram, who was looking frankly bewildered. Adrian thought that he really ought to explain, but he hardly dared open his mouth again for the moment, except to take another sip of Cognac.

Angelica evidently thought it incumbent on her, as the hostess, to fill the gap.

"It can be rather embarrassing to be able to see things that other people can't," she said, addressing Meryl directly and speaking softly, with heroic understatement. "When you're in a minority of one, as you can probably imagine easily enough, it's very easy for other people to jump to the conclusion that you're simply seeing things that aren't really there, that you're deluded, or pretending. As a child, you learn quickly enough that the best thing to do is keep quiet . . . or, at least, to be very diplomatic in your assertions. I must say that Adrian seems to have coped with that problem admirably—far better than I could when I was his age. The problem with suspicions and accusations of insanity is that they can actually drive you mad. I dread to think what kind of a mess I might be in now, if I hadn't met Jason when I did. He's been my anchor and my shield . . . and he's been a paragon of discretion, at least until now."

Jason Jarndyke blushed, presumably partly because of the compliment and partly because of the rider. "But you're no longer in a minority of one, Angie," he said, almost in a whisper. "I thought . . ."

"That remains to be proven," Angelica observed. "And as Adrian pointed out just now, talking about John Martin and Richard Dadd, not everyone who can see more than the narrow-sighted majority sees the same things. And even if we do . . . the possibility still remains that we might simply be equally deluded. Isn't that true, Adrian?"

Adrian could not know for sure whether she was talking about the elusive shadows, but the mere fact that she might be was reason enough for him to tread warily. He only hesitated for a moment. "No, Mrs. Jarndyke," he said, "I don't think that possibility would remain, if we really do see the same things. Two is the magic number. If it does turn out that your enhanced sight and mine are very similar—which is, as you say, yet to be proven—then we would no longer have any grounds for doubting that there really is something to be seen. Even if we rake up the old skepticism about knowing whether two people who have learned to call a particular color red really are having there same subjective experience of it, it doesn't alter the basic principle. If two people can agree on seeing a modification of red under the same circumstances, perhaps because their visual sensibility extends a little into what, for other people, is infra-red, then the rational response for them to adopt, even if everyone else continues to doubt, is to believe that what they're seeing is an authentic phenomenon, not a hallucination or a delusion."

"Angie thinks you're bullshitting me," Jason Jarndyke blurted out, suddenly. "Not about being a genius geneticist—she's prepared to believe that you can deliver me a Golden Fleece, of sorts—but about the other stuff. I told her what you said about the Rothko chapel, but she thinks you might be bluffing, just like I once thought she was. She doesn't want to show you any of her paintings, because she thinks you might put on an act, the way half a dozen other so-called art experts have. She doesn't want that. She claims to hate flattery, although I keep telling her that when people say she's beautiful, it's not flattery because it's the simple truth. And that's more undiplomacy in five sentences than I've dared in the last five years . . . but I'm sorry, Angie; there's only so much bottling up a man can do. And as the boy says, two is the magic number. I haven't always been able to believe you, but if he backs you up, then, as he says, there's really no more reason to doubt, is there? I honestly thought you'd be pleased. In fact, I can't understand why you're not."

Angelica had already recovered from her initial surprise and annoyance before her husband reached the end of his speech. She was looking at Adrian, not at Jason Jarndyke, trying to read his gaze—trying to figure out whether he understood why she wasn't pleased. He wasn't trying to keep anything from her, but that wasn't an issue he wanted to discuss right now, in front of two uncomprehending witnesses.

Adrian made an effort to try to look Angelica Jarndyke in the eyes, but he couldn't. He looked at Meryl Ingram instead. She was also staring at him curiously, but she was looking for an explanation of the simple fact, not its more complex ramifications, which made it a good deal easier to meet her gaze. She had blue eyes, but they were a lighter shade than his own. She had brown hair, but that was a lighter shade than his too. She was a less colorful character in more ways than one. For the moment, at least, he envied her that.

Adrian briefly considered going through the whole rigmarole that he'd spun for Jarndyke at the Savoy, but he knew that the old man would have repeated all of that to Angelica already. He thought it best to try to defuse the situation slightly by waxing philosophical, with a bit of allegory thrown in.

"The thing about the Emperor's new clothes in the famous parable," he said, addressing Meryl directly, as if he were simply endeavoring to clear up her confusion, "is that the crowd really might have been unable to see them, even if they were real, not because they were stupid, or uncultured, but because they simply didn't have the right neurophysiological equipment. Imagine the predicament of some poor fellow who, when the kid shouted out: 'The Emperor's got no clothes,' wanted to shout out: 'Yes he has, and they're beautiful! The tailors are right, and they're men of genius. That's the finest suit that any emperor ever had to wear.' What could he possibly say to convince the crowd, knowing that the majority was bound to be against him? How could he ever convince them that he really could see the suit, in all its glory, and wasn't simply crazy or—as Mr. Jarndyke might put it—bluffing? He'd be like the sighted man in H. G. Wells's 'Country of the Blind,' impotent to persuade his hosts that he was anything but a deluded fool, impending rockslide or no impending rockslide. And yet . . . perhaps the crowd should have been prepared to hear him out. They wouldn't have needed to give him the benefit of the doubt— the *admission* of doubt would have been something, in itself."

Meryl tried to make a joke out of it, also seemingly hoping to defuse the tension that had been generated without her being able to understand how or why. "I've always thought that the child in the story was a disgrace to youth," she said. "What he should have shouted was: 'Who cares whether the old fool has any clothes on or not? He's the emperor—roll out the guillotine, strike up the *Marseillaise* and full speed ahead for democracy.'"

Jason Jarndyke laughed obligingly. Angelica didn't. Adrian tried, but couldn't, although he wasn't at all sure that it wasn't a diplomatic error not to go along with the joke and allow the whole issue of who could see what to be swept under the carpet, at least for the time being, and forgotten. He tried to look at Angelica Jarndyke again. He hadn't dared study her as frankly as she'd seemed to study him, albeit briefly, when they'd first been confronted with one another, and he didn't dare to do it now, because he knew that staring at someone as beautiful as her was always a *faux pas*, but he tried to take a better measure of her, covertly.

Then he made a bold decision. He pointed at one of the panels on the wall behind her head. "That one's wrong, isn't it, Mrs. Jarndyke?" he said. "The designer did a pretty good job with the rest, but that was a slip. Maybe he couldn't find one to fit the scheme and improvised—or maybe he did it deliberately, knowing that ninety-nine people in a hundred would only see acres of brown, and that most of the one per cent wouldn't know exactly what was wrong, or why, but would just be subtly unsettled by it."

Angelica Jarndyke turned her head. She didn't have to ask him which panel he meant. "I've always thought that it was a deliberate mistake," she said, biting her lip slightly, at the risk of disturbing the gloss. "Cocking a snook, so to speak."

"I can sympathize with that," Adrian said.

She thought about it for a minute, and then nodded her head. "All right," she said. "Let's do it." Then she looked at her husband, who had set up the challenge, perhaps as if to say: *You'd better be right . . .* or perhaps not.

6

When Angelica had left the room, it suddenly seemed strangely empty to Adrian, who had not realized the extent to which she had been the one filling it. Jason Jarndyke took advantage of the natural break to suggest that they move into the drawing room, which they did, each taking an armchair upholstered—very tastefully—in brown leather.

There too, the walls were paneled in wood—and there too, Adrian immediately noticed, one of the panels had been placed in such way that the deployment of its subtle shades broke the pattern of the ensemble. Having now spotted four anomalous panels, including the two in the hallway, he was convinced that it was no coincidence. The person who had fitted the paneling could not only discriminate shades of brown that most people couldn't but had known that he could. Adrian was reluctant to believe, however, that the woodworker had been "cocking a snook," as Angelica had put it, rather quaintly. He preferred to think that the artisan had been posting a plaintive message, a fraternal gesture to others with the same ability: an amicable greeting to the likes of Angelica and himself.

But it still remained to be proven precisely how alike Angelica and he were, in terms of the extent of their vision. Ought he to believe—*dare* he believe—that she could not only see pattern anomalies in the paneling of the rooms in the Manse, but the elusive shadows?

Not that he had seen any shadows of that unique sort on his way to the Manse, and he certainly had not expected to see any inside it . . . but if they were real, and Angelica could see them too . . .

Adrian didn't want to think about that seriously until he was alone and could concentrate on the problem fully. For the moment, he was still in company with Jason Jarndyke and Meryl Ingram, and he had to concentrate his attention on making a good impression on his employer, or at least not slipping back in his estimation. No one was saying anything, for the moment, however; they were all too well aware of the fact that they were waiting, that something was about to happen. Meryl was the only one who had nothing significant at stake in that way that happening unfolded, but Adrian could see that she was aware that something was going on that she hadn't quite grasped, and he guessed that she must be able to see that, despite the fact that both he and Jarndyke were trying to feign complete relaxation, they were both secretly wound up.

How much, Adrian wondered, did Jason Jarndyke have invested in this phase of his experiment? Did he really think that it might help Angelica to feel better if she knew that there was another person close at hand who had the same ability as herself? Did he think that the knowledge might make an impact on their marriage? It was obvious, Adrian thought, that the two of them didn't dislike one another, as so many married couples seemed to, even if they had had to agree to disagree more often than they would have liked, as most married couples presumably did. He thought that they probably wanted to love one another, but didn't quite trust one another, or themselves, enough to believe that they weren't being bullshitted by the other's affectations of affection—because Angelica was, after all, a trophy wife, claimed in response to her husband's anxieties, his need to make his success manifest. On the other hand, Adrian thought, Jason surely was besotted with her beauty, and she surely was grateful to him for being her anchorage and her shield, so . . .

"That business with the panel was good," Jarndyke said, evidently feeling that the silence had lasted too long. "Clever, too. I like you, Son—I really do."

"Thanks," said Adrian, not knowing what else to say. Spotting the anomalous panel had been child's play, though. He knew that the acid test was coming up, and that even though Jarndyke did seem to like him, and had been prepared to seek him out on the basis of what his spies had told him, he wasn't yet wholly prepared to believe that Adrian had a superpower. Meryl Ingram was still at sea, even though she must have had deduced what it was that Angelica had left the dining room to fetch. Rumor must have reached her, too, that Jarndyke's wife was a painter, and she had probably been surprised on arrival that none of her works was on display.

Angelica came in to the drawing room then, carrying an easel in her right hand and a cloth-swathed canvas tucked under her left arm. Moving with meticulous orderliness, she set up the easel near a south-facing window, in order to catch the best of the late afternoon light, and placed the canvas on it, still concealed. She waited for everyone to get up from their armchairs and gather round. Then she removed the cloth.

Adrian had been half-expecting something akin to a Rothko, perhaps in shades of black, or maybe a Jackson Pollock: an exercise in abstract impressionism, playing deftly with the subtleties of color, perhaps even the utmost subtleties of color. He had not been expecting what he actually saw. He had been warned, but he had not been expecting witchcraft. He felt his jaw drop, and was uncomfortably aware that he was speechless. These, he knew, were untested waters.

He had seen a great many paintings in his time, including many by people whose color discrimination was unusually subtle, but he had never seen a painting by anyone who used color discrimination in the way that Angelica Jarndyke did, to hide images from ordinary eyes that extraordinary eyes would be able to see, if not exactly clearly and distinctly, then at least in such a way as to make out what they were.

Angelica Jarndyke was perhaps not a great draughtswoman, but she knew what it was that she was trying to represent, and how, and she had the skill to execute her plan. She was no genius, by any stretch of the imagination—no Claude Monet, no Dante Gabriel Rossetti, no Jackson Pollock—but what she had tried to do was real, and ambitious, and, in Adrian's moderately wide experience, unique.

"Now, I have to admit," said Jason Jarndyke, only half-apologetically, "that to me, that looks like just a big splodge of red with a little dash of orange here and there. Maybe it's a sunset seen in ultra-close-up, or the middle of a rose petal—and a Lancashire rose at that—but I don't get it. I don't even know why I don't like it, but I have to confess that I don't. Do you, Meryl?"

"It's more complicated than that," said Meryl. "Quite effective, in its way—disturbing, even, although I don't know exactly why. It's not an effect that I've obtained from an abstract painting before. Can you see anything that we can't, Adrian?"

"Yes," Adrian said, faintly, "I can."

"Well, what?" Jarndyke persisted. "Do you actually *like* it?"

"It's very . . . *unusual*," Adrian said, unable to think, for the moment, of a better adjective. "Technically, perhaps not completely brilliant, but in terms of coloration, in its way, it's magnificent. Magnificent, but . . ."

"But what?" This time, the prompt came from Angelica Jarndyke, who was looking at Adrian again, very intently indeed, and very impatiently.

". . . Unsettling," Adrian admitted.

Jarndyke made a noise with his tongue, like a bullshit-detector going off. "Unsettling! It's just a big splodge of red, damn it!"

"It's a depiction of Hell," Adrian said, weakly. "Or, to be precise, the Inferno—complete with the souls of the damned, in torment. Maybe I can't fully appreciate the religious context, being an atheist, but you don't need to believe in God to have a notion of Hell and retribution. The damned, I can believe in. Here, and here, and here . . . and the demons surrounding them, almost but not quite completely hidden. And the couple in the center of the picture, entwined, desperately trying to extract some consolation from their embrace . . . but failing . . . Well, as Meryl says, it really is quite disturbing, in its way . . . even for someone who can't make out the subtle figures—perhaps especially for those who can only register them subliminally. Perhaps the implication of Hell is more disturbing than the explicit depiction. But I can see the additions, and I certainly have to admit that it is unsettling."

While he was speaking, Angelica Jarndyke's expression had changed. In had lost all of its artificiality, all of its polish. She was no longer in doubt. She knew now that she hadn't just painted an illusory depiction of a private illusion that only she could see. She knew that Adrian could see the reds within the red, the souls of the damned . . . and the demons.

Which, as Adrian was all too well aware, might be unsettling in more ways than one, for both of them. He couldn't read the emotion in Angelica Jarndyke's gaze at all. There was no delight that he could see, no gratitude for being proven right, and sane, after so many years of doubt. The gaze in question abruptly shifted from Adrian to her husband, who met her stare with a bizarre expression of his own.

Adrian realized, a trifle belatedly, that a part of Angelica Jarndyke still wanted to suspect, surely in blatant defiance of all plausibility, that he'd been tipped off. She wanted, if only for a fleeting moment, to think that her husband had somehow found out what the painting represented, even though she'd probably never told him, and that he might have formed some school-boy conspiracy with Adrian to fool her.

And ironically, Jason Jarndyke seemed to be think-ing exactly the same thing. He couldn't help suspecting that perhaps his wife had somehow formed a conspiracy with Adrian, so that he could come up with an inter-pretation of the picture that she would endorse, so that the two of them could give him a slap in the eye for having doubted her.

Mercifully, they knew one another well enough, and understood one another's gaze well enough, to know, after five seconds of mutual staring, that those suspicions were utterly untenable, and rather ludicrous. Then they both turned to look at Adrian.

Adrian had thought, briefly, that if he passed the test with which Jarndyke and his wife had faced him, his employer, at least, would be delighted. He *had* passed, he knew: he had proved himself, and his uncanny sight. But Jason Jarndyke wasn't looking at him with delight. He was looking at him with confusion, like a man sud-denly afflicted by possibilities that he had previously been able to keep at bay by parrying them with the sword of doubt.

Adrian knew how he felt. The defensive wielding of the sword of doubt was a kind of fencing with which he was very familiar. His own self-satisfaction was also undermined by the sharp consciousness of knowledge that he had previously been able to keep in suspense. In spite of all the inferences he had drawn and mulled over, it was only now that he felt the full impact of the knowledge that the pitch he had made so confidently to Jarndyke a few weeks before, had been overstated.

He wasn't the only person Jason Jarndyke knew who had near-perfect color vision. Perhaps he wasn't even the best. Not only might Angelica Jarndyke be able to see better than he could, but she could paint infinitely better than he could—and, not for the first time in his life, Adrian paused to regret that he did not have the hand-eye coordination to wield a brush with as much efficacy as his sight demanded.

Except that, had he been a painter, he would not have wanted to paint Hell. And he certainly would not have wanted to paint it the strange, insidious fashion that Angelica Jarndyke had. Suddenly, being a reverse genetic engineer of genius didn't seem like such a perfect complement to his full-spectrum sight as it had seemed twenty minutes before. His ingenious argument about the emperor's new clothes and the plight of the one man in the crowd who could see the beautiful suit had ceased to be a neat philosophical argument intended for intellectual persuasion, and had taken on its full weight as a sketch of an actual, and potentially horrific, existential predicament: his own, and Angelica Jarndyke's.

Angelica Jarndyke was a painter, not of genius, but certainly of unusual talent—but no one had ever been able to see the results of her particular talent, except very vaguely, until now . . . and that had presumably shaped her decision as to what to paint, in a fashion that seemed, to say the least, ominous.

In all his esthetic excursions, Adrian had never encountered a painter capable of producing the image that had just been revealed to him. He had seen the work of a hundred painters who had real genius, and he had always thought himself better equipped to appreciate their genius than most—better than anyone else, to tell the truth—but he had never seen anything painted by someone who had elected to exploit full-spectrum sensitivity in the way that Angelica had done in her image of the Inferno, with enough skill to complement that sensitivity. Suddenly, the subject-matter seemed altogether appropriate.

Adrian knew, now, that if he did manage to produce some kind of *authentic* Golden Fleece for Jason Jarndyke, at least one person would be able to see it, consciously, in all its glory—but somehow, that idea didn't immediately fill him with delight. In fact, it frightened him, just as the revelation that he could see her work had frightened Angelica. Partly, that was just the alarm of surprise, but mainly, it was because possibilities that the two of them must both have glimpsed, but had never wanted to have to confront, were now unavoidable, and perhaps menacing.

Even so, Adrian forced himself to say: "I'd really like to see your other work some time, Mrs. Jarndyke," because he knew that he couldn't *not* say it, whether it eventually turned out to be a bad idea or not.

Jason Jarndyke was ready for that challenge, too, and showed every sign of wanting to see what Adrian would make of his wife's other works. Angelica Jarndyke seemed far more hesitant, and she made no reply to his suggestion. The silence she left dragged on, leaving everyone alone with their confusion

The true measure of Jason Jarndyke, Adrian thought—because he had to think something, in order to fill the embarrassing gap—was that he didn't seem to be jealous. He really did seem genuinely pleased, once he'd got over the initial shock, at least to know that his wife really hadn't been bullshitting him throughout their married life. He seemed to want her to be pleased, too, that she had now found someone who could see what she was doing, someone who could understand, and prove to her that she wasn't alone, and wasn't mad.

Adrian's eyes drifted back to the painting, though. A stern critic might think it a little amateurish in its technique, he supposed, but even the sternest critic, if he could actually see the image in full, would have to admit that it was brilliant, and probably unprecedented: a genuine masterpiece, in its way. But it was also a vision of Hellfire, full of wrath, complete with the souls of the damned, in agonizing torment. Adrian couldn't help wondering what Horst Koerner might make of it, if he described it to him, as requested. He made up his mind, though, almost before the thought was fully formulated that he wasn't going to ask him, or even give him a description of the image, as he could see it.

All in all, Adrian, thought, what he'd just learned would have been far less intimidating if the image had been flowers or puppies: something that might have been put on the lid of a biscuit tin back in the twentieth century; the sort of thing that trophy wives, within the scope of his admittedly limited imagination, might be expected to paint. He knew, for sure, that he was not only out of his social depth in the Old Manse, but out of his psychological depth—which troubled him far more.

Meryl Ingram seemed to be quite fascinated. Her eyes were flicking back from the painting to the faces of the other three people looking at it, measuring their various reactions just as Adrian had. To her credit, it did not seem to occur to her to challenge what Adrian has said, or even to doubt it. Indeed, she too seemed to be busy following up hypothetical possibilities in her mind, and she was the one who broke the silence once she had realized that Angelica had no intention of doing so.

"There must be other paintings like this," she said. "Undiscovered masterpieces, only visible to a few . . . unusual people. But even in familiar paintings, there must be details that most people miss—like the anomalous panel that you could see in the dining room, but I couldn't. That's remarkable—and it makes me wonder whether I'm really competent to do my job."

"Of course you are," said Adrian. "It's me who isn't. You're organizing exhibitions for people with normal sight, so you need to be able to see with normal eyes."

"That's not what you told me at the Savoy, Son," Jason Jarndyke put in, not harshly but with a hint of criticism. "You said then that even the colors people don't see consciously can be perceived subliminally. If you're right about that—about what you might eventually be able to do with the coloration and patterning of clothing—then even people who can only see Angie's painting consciously as an expanse of red might still be able to perceive its subject subconsciously, and affected by it. Isn't that so?"

Caught in his own trap, Adrian had no alternative but to acquiesce. "Yes it is," he admitted.

"And if that's the case," Meryl immediately deduced, "than part of the effect that works of art have on us, routinely, might be due to the subliminal effects of things that we *can't quite see* with our mind's eye."

"Yes," Adrian affirmed, again.

"Which throws a whole new light on the old saying: 'I don't know anything about art, but I know what I like,'" Jason Jardyke suggested, with the air of a man who had always held that intellectual standpoint.

Logically, Adrian knew, the argument was perfectly sound, and he had made it himself. But that was before he had seen the particular example constituted by Angelica Jarndyke's eccentric, unsettling masterpiece. Perhaps, as Meryl suggested, others like it existed somewhere, unexhibited and unappreciated, but they had to be exceedingly rare, and there could not be any incentive to produce them in quantity . . . except obsession.

Outside the window, dusk was falling, and the Hellfire on the easel was turning crimson, concealing its demons and enabling the torments of the damned to dissolve in a tide of blood.

Adrian looked at Angelica, and she looked back. The hurdle had been crossed and the normal flow of experience had been resumed, calm again but changed.

We need to talk, said Angelica's eyes, calmly. *But not now, and not here.*

Adrian nodded, in what he hoped was a fashion imperceptible to anyone but her.

"I'd really like to see your other work too, Mrs. Jarndyke," said Meryl Ingram, "even if I wouldn't really be able to see it."

"That can be arranged," Jason Jarndyke said, immediately, "if Angie's willing."

"Not the barn," Angelia said, immediately. "It's not ready—not finished."

"But the paintings in your old studio," Jarndyke said. "The work you did before this one. Adrian would surely like to see those—and Meryl too, even if she won't be looking at them with the same eyes. You wouldn't mind that, would you?"

Adrian got the impression that Angelica was trying very hard to work out whether she minded or not—whether, now that she knew that Adrian could actually see her work, she actually wanted it to be seen. Eventually, she said: "I suppose not. But not now. It's a mess up there. I need to sort things out, put them in order . . . arrange an exhibition of sorts. Another time."

Jason Jarndyke immediately pulled out his personal organizer, compelling everyone else to imitate him, in order that they could compare their calendars. Given that Adrian's list of future appointments was entirely blank, except for working hours, and Meryl's seemed to be very sparse, there was no difficulty in agreeing to gather again the following Sunday.

That seemed to conclude the gathering—or, more accurately, to suspend it. Thereafter, it wound down rapidly to a general leave-taking. Jason Jarndyke seemed to feel that it had been a success with regard to every item on his agenda, although he still seemed slightly troubled by his wife's initial reaction to the revelation that Adrian could see her depiction of Hell in its full detail. Adrian no longer had any idea how to evaluate the afternoon as a whole, and was glad of the opportunity to suspend his judgment, at least partially.

Although the apartment-block where Jarndyke Industries had kindly accommodated him was only a few hundred yards away, and the route was all downhill, Adrian automatically accepted Meryl Ingram's offer to give him a lift in her car. He had no hidden agenda in so doing.

7

When the car pulled up outside the apartment block Adrian fumbled momentarily with the seat-belt, which gave Meryl the opportunity to make a further attempt to strike up a conversation that she had not managed to get going during the brief downhill journey.

"Well," she said, "I've been on fix-up dates before, but nothing like that one. How was it for you?"

Adrian tried to laugh. "I'm sorry," he said. "I don't really know how these things are supposed to go. I haven't . . . haven't been on fix-up dates before, that is."

"Well, I doubt that the experience will stand you in good stead for the next time." Evidently having observed that Adrian's hand was about to turn the door-handle she said, swiftly: "Can I ask you a personal question?"

Adrian kept his hand on the handle, but didn't turn it. "Of course," he said, with what he hoped was the utmost politeness.

"This special sight," she said. "You've had a hard time with it, I assume?"

"Not really," Adrian said. "I learned quickly enough not to talk about it, and it doesn't show. I don't think it's made much difference to the way people treat me—until now, obviously, when it's become an asset in my present employment."

She didn't challenge the assertion. "But Mrs. Jarndyke seems to have had a hard time," she observed.

"Perhaps," Adrian conceded. "But that might not have anything do with her special sight. Lots of people have a hard time, for all sorts of different reasons."

She had to know that he was stonewalling, but it seemed to puzzle her rather than offend her. "If you'll forgive me saying so," she said, "you don't seem very pleased to have discovered someone else with the same ability as you—and Mrs. Jarndyke seemed positively distressed, at least for several minutes. That surprises me, I must say."

"It's probably just egotism," he lied. "We've just had proof that we're not unique."

"I don't believe that," she retorted, throwing politeness to the winds. "I really am interested in this, you know—it doesn't just impact on my profession, but my whole attitude to the things that have always engaged and fascinated me. And it isn't very flattering, by the way, that you haven't even asked me for my phone number. Even if neither of us liked one another enough to want to see one another again, there's a protocol to be observed. If you really haven't done this before, you need to learn the conventions, if only to show your boss that you're making an effort."

Adrian let go of the door handle. "I'm sorry," he said. "I really don't intend to be rude, and . . . well. I'd be a perfect fool if I didn't want to see you again, and an incompetent idiot if I didn't try to facilitate it. I was distracted. Yes, I'd like to meet again, without . . . the distractions. Maybe we can have a drink, or dinner, in Shipley some time, and actually introduce ourselves to one another in a sensible fashion. Do we really need to make a show of consulting our calendars to do that . . . assuming that you're agreeable."

"I'm agreeable," she said curtly. "Is Tuesday okay for you?"

"Yes."

"Good. You don't have a car?"

"No."

"Then I'll pick you up. Here, seven o'clock?"

Somewhat taken aback by the abruptness with which things had been organized, Adrian was only capable of a monosyllabic: "Fine." Then he took hold of the door handle again, and this time he was allowed to turn it.

When he was out of the car, he wondered whether he ought to have tried to kiss her, at least on the cheek, but decided that if the protocol had demanded it, she would probably have informed him. He was not at all sure what had just happened, or why, but he had a strong suspicion that it wasn't simply because he was, as Chester Hu put it, "pale and pretty." Whatever fascination he might have contrived to exert on Meryl Ingram was surely not simply physical. He assumed that he had become an interesting freak—which was, he thought, at least better than being an uninteresting freak, and far better than being a freak to be instinctively avoided.

It wasn't until he closed the door of the apartment behind him, and found himself in surroundings that were at least beginning to seem familiar, if not yet "home," and suddenly relaxed slightly, that he realized how tense he had been, and how much stress had built up in the course of a strange and rather awkward afternoon.

It wasn't late. That was one advantage, he supposed, to eating "dinner" at lunch-time, Yorkshire-fashion. The evening was still young. He could do some work. He could return to his routine, his own normality.

Except that, as things turned out, he couldn't. His head was still spinning. He couldn't settle down to work or to relax fully. He had too much on his mind, too much to work through.

He kept going back to the analogies that he had cited while trying to persuade Angelica Jarndyke to put him to the test. He had, of course, been putting himself in the shoes of the lone man who could see the beautiful suit, or the Wellsian sighted man in the country of the blind. Like Wells's sighted man, he had always been aware that he was sighted, not mad—not because he came from a country of the sighted, but because he had always been a scientist, at heart and in method. He had been able to subject his unusual sight to experiment and analysis, had been able to prove it to himself, at least in the basics, and to explain it to himself. He had never doubted the fact of his enhanced color perception, and he had always understood himself in that regard.

Now, though, the glimpse he had caught of Angelica Jarndyke—and the sight he had had of her fabulous painting—made him appreciate far more sharply than before, that it could have been otherwise. All the decisions he had made, with regard to handling his own predicament, still seemed logical, even in hindsight. He had known when making them that there had been alternatives, but he had simply made the decisions and concentrated on managing their consequences. He had never wasted time trying to calculate the possible consequences of the decisions he had *not* taken. Now, he felt compelled to think about that a little more deeply, and to extend his analysis. He didn't suppose that he could work out how Angelica Jarndyke had seen her situation, and how she had tried to cope with it, but at least he could ask himself what might have happened to *him* if he had tried to go in a different direction.

Suppose, he thought, that he *had* doubted himself. Suppose that the fact that other people couldn't see what he saw had obliged him to doubt that he saw it, rather than providing the stimulus to prove it. Suppose that he had been able to reproduce what he saw, with the aid of artificial pigments, at least to the extent that available artificial pigments would allow—but that people still couldn't see what he saw, or even that there're was anything there to see? Might he have actually stopped seeing it? Might he have adapted and amended his consciousness to what other people could see, psychosomatically rendering himself partially blind?

Yes, he decided, he might. And perhaps some people did. Perhaps it wasn't simply an accident of fate or physiology that so many people who were affected by color weren't conscious of the effects or discriminations they were making. Perhaps it was a psychosomatic compulsion, driven by the need that so many people had to fit in, to be normal . . . a need by which Adrian had never been unduly afflicted, having always thought it better to be a scientist, a man of logic rather than emotion, and having long ago given up on the possibility of ever *fitting in*.

On the other hand, might he have been able to cling to the conviction that he really could see, and really could reproduce what he saw, even though other people couldn't see the reality or the reproduction—but without the scientific understanding that would inform him as to how it came about, and the practical means to explore that genesis, with the aid of practical genomics, and the multitudinous possibilities of contemporary genetic engineering?

Yes, he decided, he might. And surely some people had, long before Angelica Jarndyke. Maybe only a few, maybe more than a few. And might they not, given the conviction without the scientific understanding, have construed what they possessed and could do in consequence as a kind of magic, a kind of witchcraft? Might they not have come to believe that their difference from other people really was a kind of superpower: something in frank defiance of normality, simultaneously a boon and a curse?

Watch out for Medea, Adrian thought. *Okay. I watched out. I met her. But what now? What now?*

What he meant by that, of course, was what might Angelica Jarndyke want of him, now that she had found him? And what might Jason Jarndyke want of him now, not as a genomic engineer charged with the job of revolutionizing the coloration of his fabrics, but as a "member of the family," who shared his wife's peculiar vision? But even those two questions, difficult as they were, were only half the problem.

The other half was the question of what he might want himself, given the sudden change in his circumstances, and whether it would undermine all the sterling work he had put into shaping his attitude, planning his career and delineating his goals.

What if Angelica Jarndyke's paintings really could work a kind of magic on him, and show him something new, something disturbing? What if his extraordinary sight, which had already given him a privileged glimpse of her vision of Hell, were to show him something even more unsettling, which he might be better off not seeing?

The possibilities seemed too confusing for there to be any hope of formulating a strategy in advance. But one set of questions stood out: Assuming that she could see them, had Angelica painted the elusive shadows? Had she at least tried? And if she had tried, had she actually managed to get them into focus, to perceive their design and their structure? Had she, with the aid of her particular talent as a painter, been able to produce a depiction sufficiently detailed and sufficiently accurate to allow a scientifically trained eye to make progress in the task of working out what on earth the damned things might actually *be*, and whether their existence and nature were of any relevance to the human beings who could not see them, or at least to those who could?

Had that been the kind of thinking behind the look that Angelica Jarndyke had given him, which had seemed to signify: *We need to talk?* He didn't know. He didn't know for sure that Angelica could see the fleeting shadows, or what it might imply if she couldn't, and if he had then to conclude that they, at least, were a mirage produced by his own unconscious—or, on the other hand, what it might imply if she could, and if their objective reality were established, even while their nature remained frustratingly elusive?

He had spent years telling himself that the anomalous shadows, even if they were real, were essentially irrelevant, that they were only shadows: visual phenomena, devoid of materiality. And he had surely been right. But always, underneath that assurance, there had been the further suspicion: that if they really were shadows of a sort, then they must be the shadows *of* something, albeit something exceedingly strange, and even more elusive than the elusive shadows themselves.

I really do need to talk to her, he thought. *I need to talk to her in private, without Jayjay looking on. I need to find out what she sees and what she knows, to find out whether there's anything that will permit a better understanding of what the hell they are. And she needs to talk to me for exactly the same reason. We both need it, even if it turns out that neither of us knows anything more than the other, and that the shadows are eluding us both to exactly the same frustrating extent. One way or the other, we need to know.*

With that train of thought running through his mind, he assumed, when his phone bleeped in his pocket, that it was Angelica Jarndyke ringing to arrange the meeting—which she would have to do, because he hadn't asked her for her phone number, whereas she could easily get his from Jayjay's organizer.

In fact, though, it wasn't Angelica. It was Jason Jarndyke.

"I just wanted to thank you for coming," his employer said, "and ask how you got on with Meryl."

"Fine," said Adrian. "We made a date for Tuesday."

"Wow," said Jarndyke. "You don't hang about, do you? Well done, Son. I knew you two would hit it off."

"It was kind of you to introduce us," Adrian said, obligingly. "And the meal was excellent." He left it at that, figuring that it was up to Jarndyke to introduce the real reason that he had called.

"You're welcome," Jarndyce said, and added: "Angie's in the barn. I don't know what she's painting in there, because she won't let me in, but I don't suppose I'd be able to see anything if she did. I'm grateful to you, too. I really wasn't sure, you see. I always wanted to believe her, but I could never quite persuade myself. You've taken a load off my mind. And I'm sure she'll be grateful too. If she seemed a bit stunned earlier, it's because she couldn't quite believe me when I told her that you were like her. She was never quite able to believe in herself, you see. Now, she can. It'll be a load of her mind too, I'm sure. I'm really glad that it all worked out—for us for you, for everyone."

"Me too," said Adrian, wishing that he could be certain that it had all "worked out" . . . or, indeed, that anything had.

108

8

By the time that Adrian got to work the following morning normality appeared to have been restored, even though his work routine was not sufficiently established to qualify as completely familiar. An interval of sleep had fully restored his ability to concentrate on his work, and he threw himself into it with what he liked to think of as his typical ardor, shelving all other issues in favor of the marvelously detailed and orderly business of genetic tinkering and the synthesis of colors.

It was mid-afternoon before Jason Jarndyke appeared in his lab, once again showing a mysterious ability to calculate exactly when he would be waiting for an experimental run to reach its conclusion and produce the result necessary to facilitate the next step in his marathon quest for the golden fleece.

"It seems that I was a bit premature when I rang you at home last night," Jarndyke told him, without any preliminaries.

"Really?" Adrian queried.

"As I said, I hadn't really believed—not complete-ly—that you would be able to see anything in Angie's picture that I couldn't, and I have to admit that I wasn't immediately convinced that what you thought you saw was what she thought she had put into it. It was overly suspicious of me, I know, but I couldn't help thinking that she might be going along with what you said in or-der to prove to me that she'd been telling me the truth all along . . . but that's by the by. What I *had* taken for granted was that if you did see something, which she really had put into it, that she'd be pleased. I thought she'd be over the moon at being able to prove to me— or at least put up a good argument to the effect—that she really hadn't been bullshitting me all these years. I thought she'd be grateful. When she didn't show it immediately, I thought it was just the shock."

"But it wasn't?" Adrian inferred, without difficulty.

"Well, seemingly not. You've probably heard, the rumor mill being what it is, that she has bouts of de-pression. Bad bouts, sometimes. Maybe it's just a co-incidence, and has nothing to do with what happened yesterday, but she was in the barn for a long time last night, and when she finally came out . . . well, she hasn't got out of bed all day, and it certainly isn't just a matter of needing sleep. I wanted to call a doctor, but she wouldn't have it . . . never will. I'm at a loss, quite honestly. I really thought she'd be glad, happy, even. I don't understand it at all."

"It must have been a shock," Adrian ventured, mildly. "Sometimes, shock causes a physical reaction. Clinical depression isn't necessarily a symptom of unhappiness."

"I know. Believe me, I've looked it up—not to mention down and endwise. But I've thought about her likely reaction to the revelation that you could see her picture, and the corollary conclusion you'll be able to see what's in her other pictures too, both the ones I've seen and the ones she won't let me see. I think that scares her, a little. She'd got used to it, you see—people not being able to see, only praising her work, if and when they did, purely for reasons of bluff. She'd got used to painting with the assumption that no one else would be able to see what she was painting. Now, the thought that someone *can* see . . . *will* see . . . has taken her aback a bit, given her pause for thought. I'm sure she'll come round, though."

"I don't want to cause any difficulty. If she'd rather I didn't come on Sunday . . ."

"Difficulty?" Jarndyke echoed, interrupting him. "No, Son, there's no difficulty. In my book, you're still a godsend. You have no idea how much she needs you . . . needs an audience, that is, who can see and understand what she's doing. It'll complete her . . . when she can get her head around it properly."

"I don't know about that, Mr. Jarndyke . . ." said Adrian, warily.

"Jayjay. Neither does she, at present—but she'll come round. It's what she needs—what she's always needed. You must understand that."

He was evidently looking for reassurance, desperately in need of an endorsement of his judgment. Unfortunately, Adrian wasn't at all sure that he could provide one—not honestly, at any rate.

"I'll be glad to help, if I can," he said, thinking that it was a safe enough offer.

"Thanks, Son," Jarndyke said. "I'll let you know." Then, abruptly, as if pulling himself together with a supreme effort, he changed his attitude and his tone. "Don't get any ideas, mind," he said, putting on a grotesquely contrived humorous expression again. "You're a nice looking lad and she's beautiful, but she's damn near old enough to be your mother, and she towers over you. You might think she's only with me for my money, but even if you were right . . . oh, don't blush like that. I'm not entirely color blind, and I know what some red splodges mean. What I'm trying to say is that she's only ever going to be interested in your eyes, and you need to understand that, and not get confused, the way youngsters sometimes do. Because I want this to work, Son—I really do. I adore Angie, and I want her to have what I've never been able to give her: the sight of your eyes. That's worth more to me than the Golden Fleece itself. In fact, if we're being metaphorical, that *is* my authentic Golden Fleece. If you can give me genes to produce colors that can live up to your promises, that might well complete my material fortune . . . but if you can give Angie faith in her work, and faith in herself, and set her free from the disappointment, anguish and depression that's been dogging her for years . . . well, Son, you'll have worked a real miracle."

Adrian thought that he could actually feel his heart sinking. He had thought, a week before, that he could justify all the hopes that Jason Jarndyke had invested in him—but the game had changed now. Now, the

Yorkshireman was expecting miracles. Adrian was a scientist; he didn't do miracles. He couldn't even bring himself to say that he would do his best. He would, but he knew that it wouldn't be enough.

"You're still blushing, you silly sod," Jarndyke observed. "But you see what I'm getting at, don't you? She hasn't got used to the idea yet, but she will. Bound to. I can't ask you to dinner again before Sunday, obviously—I'll have to wait for her to ask me to invite you, if she does. But Sunday's definitely on, even if she decides that she doesn't want to show you more of her work just yet. Eventually, she will . . . and even if it takes months, one day, she'll want to take you into the barn to see what she's doing at present. Just your eyes, mind, and your consciousness behind them. No daft ideas—but she'll want you to see . . . and *I* want you to see. Need to be clear about that." He hesitated, apparently wondering whether he might have gone too far—but real self-doubt wasn't in his emotional repertoire. "Not saying that you can work a miracle, mind," the industrialist added, cautiously, "and I won't hold it against you if you can't—but the mere possibility justifies the price of your hire . . . metaphorically speaking, of course. You up to date now?"

Adrian blinked several times, and then nodded.

"We're on the same page?" Jarndyke added, wanting to be sure.

Adrian nodded again.

"Good—now get on with making me trillions. Concentrate on your own colors, until Sunday, unless you get the call before. Okay?"

"Okay," said Adrian, feeling that the nodding was becoming too repetitive, and not wanting to be mistaken for an automaton.

"Champion," said Jarndyke, and passed on.

Word that the conversation in question had taken place went round the labs and offices like wildfire, although no one knew *exactly* what had been said or why. Rumor inevitably took wing.

"Made quite an impression on Mrs. Jarndyke, I hear," Chester Hu said to him, when an opportunity arose. "I told you to be careful, didn't I? Don't be fooled by Jayjay's easygoing manner. If he gets jealous, he won't settle for firing you. He's a Yorkshireman—the next worst thing to a Singaporean, when it comes to matters of the heart."

The Koreans, the Taiwanese, and even the lone Scot, the other Englishman and the Austrian made similar comparisons, causing Adrian to realize that every nation on Earth thought that it had a privileged relationship with jealousy and pride.

"Don't worry about it, though," Martin Rutledge advised him, in contrast to Chester Hu. "His bark's worse than his bite, and he can control himself. Did he try to fix you up yesterday?"

"Yes," Adrian admitted.

"Are you seeing her again?"

"Yes—tomorrow."

"God, you're a fast worker. That's great, then, Screw her, whoever she is, and think about Angelica, if you must . . . but make sure that Jayjay knows who it is you're screwing. Everything will be fine."

114

Horst Koerner was less optimistic. "Troubled waters, my friend," he said. "Deep forces of the unconscious at work. Tread carefully. Did you see her pictures?"

"Only one," Adrian confessed, warily.

"Describe it."

"Difficult to describe," Adrian said, figuring that it wasn't entirely a lie. "Mostly red. Lots of red."

"Blood red?"

"Some—it depended on the light. More once the sun was going down."

"Well, you're supposed to be the expert on the psychological significance of color. You can interpret the symbolism as well as I can. She's a passionate woman, and Jayjay's not getting any younger. Treat her gently, though, if she does fixate on you. Hell hath no fury, etcetera. Feign innocence and duck. It will pass."

Adrian's first thought in response to that avalanche of nonsense was that it was quite unnecessary for him to feign innocence, but he certainly had no intention of telling Horst Koerner that.

He brushed off all the unwanted attention—which didn't fan the rumors, but didn't extinguish them either. He now felt that it wasn't just Jason Jarndyke's beady eyes that were on him, but those of the entire organization.

Mercifully, he had his routines, and a heroic capacity to absorb himself in his work. That was what he did on Tuesday, taking the progress of his gene-designing, gene-manufacturing and gene-implanting experiments one small step further, looking forward to the day when he could actually begin field-testing. For the moment, except for the experiments in progress he'd brought with him from Imperial, which had already produced numerous splashes of color in flasks and Petri dishes, he was mostly working in cyberspace and headspace, where the hitches rarely showed up, but he had already set projects in motion to get half a dozen new pigment genes—all patent-protected—into organic form, and to incorporate them into cultures of both wool and silk. Within a fortnight, if all went well, he would begin to see further flecks of new color born in his Petri-dishes, to complete the spectrum launched at Imperial, and he would know that the foundations had been solidly laid for a great ideative and industrial enterprise.

He allowed himself to feel a small thrill of triumph, but not to celebrate. The time for celebration was still a long way off.

For the moment, it looked as if his reds, greens and blues would start coming in way ahead of his golds, but he wasn't upset by that. The golds would come through, in time; so would the blacks . . . and the violets too. They would only be splodges in dishes to begin with, but in time . . . maybe he could even produce Hellfire, if there turned out to a market for it.

His progress thus far seemed elementary, and frustratingly slow, because his ambitions were so large, but he knew that Jason Jarndyke was right. Rome hadn't been built in a day, and the Romans hadn't made as great a job of it as they might have done, although the Goths and Vandals certainly hadn't helped with its preservation. He knew that he had to be patient.

He was. He worked with relentless efficiency all day, by no means tirelessly, but effectively. Everything went like clockwork, uninterrupted by superfluous cuckoos. He had plenty to think about without undue philosophizing, and he made the most of his opportunities. His head was full of molecules.

He got home at six-fifteen, just in time to shower and change, to get ready for the first real date he had ever had, slightly anxious about his ignorance of the protocols, but not having sufficient emotional investment in the plan to worry unduly about the possibility of everything going disastrously wrong.

Meryl was very punctual, which he decided to accept as a good augury. Without consulting him, she drove him to a restaurant high in the moors, where she had taken the precaution of reserving a table. He reminded himself that she was a professional organizer, in whom such habits were doubtless already ingrained. He had no objection at all.

9

"I read your articles on-line," Meryl told him, in between plying her fork, chewing pasta and taking delicate sips from her wine-glass. "They're not exactly in high profile locations."

"No, they're not," Adrian agreed, between his own gustatory punctuation marks. "Save for a couple of the more tedious ones, I didn't write them in order to pad out my official publications record, more for the sake of personal interest."

"But it's interesting work. The web is so vast, and navigating it is so difficult, that so much stuff simply gets lost in the wilderness. I realize that the applications of your thinking to matters of art aren't your priority, but to me they're extremely interesting. Is there more, that you haven't yet got around to typing up?"

"Some," Adrian admitted. "Some of it I can't publish, and quite a lot I'll probably never get around to publishing, but I'll continue to visit galleries whenever I can, and I'll doubtless keep finding new points of interest. You can be sure I'll be at all the exhibitions you put on at the Mill, and anything that's on in Leeds or York."

"When you say that there's stuff you can't publish, do you mean that it's too closely related to the work you're doing for Jarndyke?"

"No—just stuff that I can't publish."

"I don't understand. Why wouldn't you be able to publish it?"

Adrian hesitated. Strictly speaking, even talking to Meryl Ingram constituted publication of a sort, but he was on a date, and he wanted to impress her, so he decided to let her in on the secret. "A couple of years back, while I was in London, I began to study the subtle metamorphoses of pigments over time. It's not exactly radioactive dating, but once you know what you're looking for—always provided that you can see it, which most people can't—you can use the alterations in the pigments to date pictures with a reasonable degree of accuracy."

For a moment, she seemed puzzled, and then enlightenment dawned. "You're saying that you can detect fakes more accurately than the supposed experts?"

"Not all fakes—just fakes produced some time after the death of the supposed artist. I've become quite good at spotting a lot of them almost at a glance. The problem is, of course, that it's not a recognized method, and I'm not a recognized expert, and nobody would believe that my eyesight is capable of making the relevant discriminations if they had a vested interest in refusing to believe it. And if people did believe me, it would be even worse. So I don't tell people—until now."

"I'm grateful to be the exception. Why would it be worse if people believed you, though?"

"Because there are a great many people who have a great deal of money invested in the supposed certainty that the paintings they own are genuine. If any expert using an accredited method can tell that a painting is a fake, there's nothing much the owner can do to challenge the general judgment, but if it's only one man, possessed of a means of discrimination that no one else has . . . well, you can follow the logic." He drew a forefinger cross his throat.

She hadn't actually needed the gesture to catch his drift. Her eyebrows were already raised, not in shock but in admiration.

"In any case," Adrian added, "I can't really see that anybody gains from the revelation that a painting long certified as genuine is really a fake. The owner, any auction house that sells it, and even the public who go to look at it in a gallery, all have an interest in believing that it's the real thing—and quite honestly, if nobody but me can tell the difference, it's obviously as good as the real thing so far as everybody else is concerned, so why burst the bubble of illusion? So, I have no intention of hiring myself out as a consultant, and no intention of publicizing the fact that I can do it. You don't have to worry about the Mill, by the way—because Hockney was still alive when the gallery was established, he was able to certify the material that went into it at the time, and it's less than fifty years since he died, so any fakes of his works that have crept in since wouldn't be detectable with any degree of certainty."

"But the special exhibitions . . ." she began, and then stopped. She frowned.

"Precisely," said Adrian. "It wouldn't be in your interest to ask me, or mine to tell you. Let sleeping paint lie . . . in more ways than one."

"It doesn't matter," she concluded, after a moment's thought. "What I'm really interested in, for professional reasons, is the topic you introduced at the Jarndykes' place: the different eyesights that different artists might, or must, have had. Back in the last century, ophthalmologists were able to identify the specific eye trouble by which Turner was afflicted, and various analysts were able to produce evidence as to which painters in the past had made use of a *camera obscura* or various optical instruments, but there's obviously enormous scope there for someone with your ability. That, presumably, is the kind of work you *could* publish, but would probably never get round to?"

"True," Adrian admitted.

"But you wouldn't object to publication, for instance, by a collaborator . . . and I do mean a collaborator, not someone simply ripping off your work? Someone who could make a meaningful contribution of her own?"

Adrian smiled. "No," he said, "I wouldn't have any objection to that at all. In fact, I'd be quite grateful to find someone like that, who could complement my work and formulate it . . . and perhaps even publish in more prominent web locations than I contrived myself, in my desultory fashion."

Adrian saw that she seemed mildly surprised. She hadn't expected it to be that simple. "I'd be getting more advantage out of it that you would," she said, warily. "When I say that I wouldn't be ripping you off, maybe that's true, strictly speaking . . . but I would be exploiting you."

"No, you wouldn't," he said. "You'd be helping me to get something done that I'd probably never get round to doing myself—something interesting. If it helps you too, in your career, so much the better."

She studied him, apparently trying to decide whether he really meant it or not. By the time the dessert was served, though, she seemed convinced, even though she still seemed to be surprised by the casual way in which he had accepted her proposal.

"Mrs. Jarndyke is very impressive, isn't she?" she observed. "I don't think I've ever been so close to such a beautiful woman. Even in her forties, she made me look positively dowdy."

"Not at all," Adrian said, as he was doubtless supposed to do. "But you must see hundreds of beautiful women in your line of work. I'm the one for whom it was a genuinely novel experience. I've led a sheltered life in that regard. Not that female geneticists are plain, of course, but . . . well, I've always been deeply absorbed in my work. The meal at the Old Manse was like nothing I've ever been called upon to do before— quite nerve-racking, in its way. You must have business lunches all the time."

"Not really," she said. "You seem to be overestimating my status, as Jarndyke did, if he really did invite me because he wants to talk to me about organizing an exhibition of the history of Yorkshire textiles. That's above my pay grade at present—although boosting my publications record, with your help, might advance

122

my status somewhat, hopefully soon enough to step into my boss's shoes when she leaves. She'll be the one organizing his exhibition, though, if there is one. She'll probably jump at the chance. I'll just be the errand girl."

"As Angelica said, I'm sure your day will come. I've been extraordinarily lucky in getting my golden opportunity so soon."

"Hardly," said Meryl. "Reports of your genius certainly don't seem to be exaggerated. Having to compare myself looks-wise to Angelica and to you intellectually really put me in my place on Sunday. Out of my depth is putting it mildly."

"You shouldn't sell yourself short," Adrian said, dutifully. "Mr. Jarndyke did invite you—he must think you have potential. He's not a stupid man."

"You don't have to spare my feelings. Everyone in Shipley knows that he's always fishing for women to introduce to his new recruits. He doesn't pick them because of their titanic intellect, or their stunning looks. He just tries to match their interests. I got lucky because you like hanging around in art galleries. Still, it *was* lucky." She paused deliberately before adding: "I got an easy path to some potentially useful publications, and I even get to go back again next Sunday for more good wine and a look at some more seriously weird paintings."

Unsure as to how to reply to that, Adrian remained silent, occupying himself with his coffee cup.

After a pause, Meryl sat back in her chair, and drained the last of the coffee from her own cup. "Well,

I guess I owe Jason Jarndyke one," she said. "Best fix-up date I ever had, by a long way. I'll lay odds that none of the other girls he's pimped to his hot shots even got a decent fuck out of it."

Adrian blinked, repeatedly.

"Sorry," she said. "Didn't mean to shock you—forgot about the sheltered upbringing. I'm even looking forward to seeing Angelica again, even if she does make me look a dog's arse by comparison—don't bother with the polite denial; I know my limitations. She's a fascinating woman. I'll be interested to see . . . or at least hear . . . what you make of her other paintings, especially if they're as off-beat as the one we saw. Do you think we'll get a further invitation for the following week, to see what's in that mysterious barn of hers?"

"I suspect not," said Adrian. "It's work in progress—she probably won't want anyone to see it until it's finished, and that might take a long time. I only caught a glimpse of the outbuilding on Sunday, but even though it's not really a barn, it's a big shed. If she's painting murals, it could take years."

"If it were you, and you could paint, what would you be doing in there?"

"God knows. I'd be an entirely different person. How can I tell?"

"I don't know. But I do know that you wouldn't have painted that Inferno picture."

"Why not?"

"You're not that kind of person."

"And Angelica is?"

"Obviously—but you wouldn't think it to look at her, would you?"

"Perhaps I am too, but it's just that you wouldn't think it to look at me."

"It's different. You're an innocent, an open book. She's not just a woman, but an uncommonly beautiful one, for whom honesty is impossible."

"That's a bit harsh."

"No, it's not. I might be dowdy by comparison, but I understand the logic of the situation—the situation of being the permanent focus of all the lascivious gazes in the world, that is. No one can endure that without building a false face, a false identity. Beauty is only mask-deep, but as to what's inside . . . who can tell? In her case, apparently, hellfire and damnation."

"It's only one picture. It might be part of a set, with a counterpart in pastel greens representing Paradise."

"It's the picture she chose to show you—not us, but you, specifically. She might not really have believed that you'd be able to see it until you gave her the proof, but she certainly knew that if you could see it, you'd be the only one. If all her others are pleasant dreams and cute puppy dogs, it would only make it more significant that she picked out that one for you."

Adrian remembered Horst Koerner's invitation to consider the symbolism of blood.

"It was just a test," he said. "She wasn't tacitly committing me to damnation and eternal torment."

"Don't pretend to be more ingenuous than you are, Adrian. Of course she wasn't committing you to the flames of Hell—she was trying to tell you that it's where she is, metaphorically speaking . . . or maybe where she would be, without Jarndyke. Did she come to see you on her own last night?"

Adrian started slightly. "No—what makes you think that she might have done?"

"I might not be able to see the way you can, but I'm not blind. Maybe she'll wait until after Sunday, when you've seen the rest of her juvenilia, but she'll come, believe me. I just can't quite figure out *why*. I understand the logic of the situation, I think, but the way the pair of you reacted on Sunday . . . the demons and the souls of the damned in the sea of blood and fire weren't the only things not meeting the eye. I could almost believe that she had designs on your body, but I don't think she'd do that to her husband . . . I don't mean that she wouldn't cheat on him, obviously—she's a woman, after all—but that she wouldn't imperil his relationship with the man who's supposedly going to make him, and therefore her, billions."

"You're refreshingly cynical," Adrian observed. "These northerners are a little lacking in that kind of southern vitriol, don't you think?"

"And you're refreshingly uncynical," she countered. "It's hard to believe that you've been living in London for . . . what is it? Six years?"

"Seven—but very reclusively. Married to my work hardly begins to describe it."

Adrian could see that another smart rejoinder was hovering on her lips, but she paused, and then said: "You know what it is, don't you? You know what it is that's tormenting her, I mean. That's why you're avoiding the subject. But if it's a side-effect of the special sight, why isn't it tormenting you?"

"How do you know that it isn't? Perhaps I'm not as easy to read as you think."

"Don't be silly. If I had to bet, I'd say that this was the first date you've been on in at least seven years, and yet you're, if not ice-cold, at least cucumber-cool. Presumably you don't care what kind of impression you make on me, which isn't very flattering, but it also means that you're a hell of a lot more at ease with yourself than Angelica Jarndyke is. You must at least have a suspicion of what's bugging her, though. Curiouser and curiouser, as Alice would say. But I'm glad I bullied you into taking me out. I assume we're splitting the bill? That's the protocol, if you don't know."

Until Meryl had stated the opposite in so many words, Adrian had not actually realized how much, in fact, he *did* care what kind of impression he made on her—and not simply for reasons of personal pride, or because they were apparently going to collaborate on the completion of various aborted art projects. He was glad that he hadn't previously brought that concern to the forefront of consciousness, where it would have undermined his contrived coolness considerably.

It was not simply the awareness in question that devastated his coolness, however, as they walked back to the car and she suddenly said: "Your place or mine?" and then added, when he made no reply: "Mine I suppose. I bet you don't even have a double bed."

Adrian swallowed his saliva. "You don't have to . . ." he stuttered.

"I know I don't have to, idiot," she said. "I'm not offering you a *quid pro quo* for consenting so meekly

127

to helping me further my career, I'm following my wayward whim—and trying to figure out whether your astonishing neglect of flattery really reflects a total lack of interest. That would be hard to bear. Oh good . . . embarrassment at last. Get in, damn it, and fasten your seat belt."

Adrian got into the car, and fastened his seat belt.

Contrary to Martin Rutledge's advice, and perhaps all likelihood, he did not think about Angelica Jarndyke while he and Meryl Ingram eventually came to grips, but it was his first time, and he was unaware of the protocol.

10

Dinner the following Sunday went reasonably smoothly, aided by the fact that, by that time, Adrian was thoroughly besotted with Meryl, and could not help allowing it to show, just a little—seemingly enough, at any rate, to delight Jason Jarndyke, who had obviously been hoping to see it, although not enough to awaken the slightest hint of interest in Angelica. Angelica, however, did not give the impression that anything short of an earthquake would awaken the slightest hint of any emotional reaction in her. Her mask of beauty was perfect, but she seemed to have suffered a complete loss of affect behind it.

Jason Jarndyke had dropped in on Adrian in the laboratory the day before to assure him that his wife was completely recovered from her fit of depression and was busy preparing the private exhibition of her painting, but his notion of "completely recovered" obviously contained a significant dose of optimism. Angelica did not seem sad, or even fatigued, but she did seem quite vacant. She made a tokenistic effort to contribute to the conversation, but her remarks were conspicuously anodyne, and the bulk of the chatter during the various courses of the meal was orchestrated and provided by her husband and Meryl.

Adrian featured more frequently as a topic of that conversation than a contributor, once the two of them had exhausted the topic of the hypothetical exhibition that Meryl was never really going to organize. They seemed to by vying, then, in proffering complimentary accounts of different aspects of his intellect, albeit with a distinct whiff of irony on Meryl's part. Adrian sought to meet Angelica's gaze more than once in search of a hint of conspiratorial sympathy, but failed.

Jarndyke apparently became aware, eventually, that his interchanges with Meryl were causing Adrian more embarrassment than pleasure, and decided that he ought to address him directly rather than singing his praises obliquely.

"I noticed on your CV that you went to a GRE conference in Oslo back in '59," he remarked. "Did you take in Gustav Vigelund's sculpture park? The *Vita?*"

"Of course," Adrian said. "Not really my cup of tea, though. A bit austere. Colorless. Impressive, but . . . just not my sort of thing."

"I liked it," Jarndyke said, blithely. "What about the other brother? Did you visit *his Vita?*"

That was the point of the question, Adrian realized. Jason Jarndyke was fishing. Gustav Vigelund's little brother Emmanuel had not been given a park in which to show off. He had been an official recorder, painting portraits of local dignitaries to hang in civic buildings, condemned to a humdrum existence of conspicuous underachievement, living in an ordinary house on an ordinary estate—until he had ripped out all the floors in his ordinary house and made the entire interior into a single coherent space, on whose black-dyed walls he'd painted his own all-encompassing vision of human life, in all its aspects, which was designed to be looked at in dim light, so that visitors had to be in there for a good half hour before their eyes adjusted sufficiently to see it as it was meant to be seen.

A blind man could have spotted the hidden agenda. Jason Jarndyke had obviously formed his own hypothesis about what was going on in Angelica's "barn"—either that or he had actually taken a surreptitious look inside. Doubtless Angelica had once "dragged" him to see Emmanuel's house, which was only open to the public for a couple of hours a week, perhaps because the local authorities considered his *Vita* to be shamefully pornographic.

"Yes," Adrian said. "I saw it."

"And what did you think?" was the inevitable next question.

"Original. Ingenious. Very effective. A masterpiece, in its way."

"Not brilliant? Not a work of genius?"

"Maybe not entirely my cup of tea," Adrian hedged. "More so than Gustav's *Vita*, certainly, but still . . . in sum, less than my particular eye could have desired to see."

"Angie liked it," Jarndyke said, laying down the hook along with the lure.

She bit, but almost dutifully, because it was expected of her—or so Adrian thought. "Dr. Stamford's right," she said, colorlessly. "It's a masterpiece, in its way. Original, ingenious and effective . . . but it uses semi-darkness as a cloak, to shield its weaknesses. I can sympathize with that, I suppose, but . . . well, I did like it, but not as much as the Rothko chapel. Rothko could use near-black in a way that Vigelund junior couldn't. Rothko understood its subtleties better."

It wasn't really a lead-in, but Jarndyke used it anyway.

"Angie has some pictures set up in the library that she'd like to show you," he said to Adrian. "To demonstrate that she *does* understand near-black . . . as well as red and blue . . . and maybe even gold."

"If only I were a genetic engineer instead of a mere dauber, darling," his wife retorted, a trifle sharply, "what sweet music we might make . . . not to mention money. I fear that my paintings are never going to find much of a market."

"That doesn't matter," Jarndyke said, affectionately. "What matters is that *you* know what they're worth."

"I'm sure that Mrs. Jarndyke has always known that," Adrian put in, trying to be gallant even though he knew that it was definitely not one of his talents. "I'll be very interested to see them. I've been looking forward to it immensely."

"It's only a small sample of the total though," Jarndyke put in. "Old stuff, I believe. All her recent work is in the barn. I haven't seen any of it—she gave up asking for my opinion years ago. I can't blame her for that, though."

All that Angelica said in reply to that was: "It's not really a barn, Jayjay. It's just an outbuilding. No live-stock, no tractor, no bales of hay. My paintings are just amateurish dabbling—not worth seeing, really. I wish you wouldn't go on about it so."

"Sorry, Angie," Jarndyke said, contritely, although he must have known that her under-evaluation of her endeavors was blatantly insincere.

"And it's not a rip-off of Emmanuel Vigelund either, so you can give up on that guess," she said. "It's not a collective vision of human life, pornographic or other-wise, to be seen in quiet light as if in a church."

"Can't blame a fellow for wondering," Jarndyke said. "Are we going to the library, or what?"

"No," said Angelica, suddenly stern. "*We* aren't. Dr. Stamford, Miss Ingram and I are going to the library. *You* are going to stay here, Jason. This doesn't concern you."

That did not seem fair to his employer, and Adrian detected more than a hint of resentment in the way that Jarndyke replied: "You called them Adrian and Meryl last week—why so formal all of a sudden?"

That seemed a trifle unfair to Adrian, too, especially as Jason Jarndyke had hardly ever addressed him as "Adrian" or "Dr. Stamford" since their first meeting at the Savoy but almost invariably as "Son." He resisted the temptation to intervene on either side, though, and meekly allowed Angelica Jarndyke to escort him and Meryl out of the room and along the wood-paneled corridor that presumably led to the library.

The library really was pretending to be an antique library, with laden bookshelves containing nothing but printed books. The room had no screens and no electronic storage devices. As works of art went, however, it was conspicuously fake—conspicuous, at least, to any genuine reader. The most superficial inspection of the spines permitted the conclusion that books had been purchased by the meter and arranged in accordance with the styles of the bindings, with no intention that they would ever be opened. Some were in foreign languages, including Welsh and Latin, others were nineteenth-century religious texts or sets of classic authors of a similar vintage. Adrian did not waste any time examining the contents of the shelves in detail, however. He was infinitely more interested in the paintings.

There were seven, each set up on its own easel, the L-shaped array carefully spaced, as if the intervals had been measured with a ruler.

Like the vision of Hellfire he had already seen, he saw at a glance that they would have looked like mere "splodges" to the everyday eye, and presumably looked like exactly that to Meryl. Like the vision of Hellfire, though, they were not, in fact, essays in abstract impressionism. They were representative pictures of a sort—very subtle pictures, using delicate gradations of color, but representative nevertheless. Some of them needed careful study, even by his subtle eye, but there was not one that left Adrian confused as to its subject.

The order in which the seven pictures had been set out was not that of the colors of the spectrum, and

Adrian detected soon enough that it was not the order of their composition either, and wondered whether the sequence had been mixed up deliberately, as a further small test of his judgment. Although the seven showed clear traces of an evolution of skill and technique, the series did not start with the most primitive and lead to the most sophisticated. Having walked along the entire L, scanning each item briefly, Adrian quickly concluded that all seven pre-dated the vision of Hell, and that the earliest of them, perhaps Angelica's first venture in "invisible painting," was the study in yellow, whose shades varied from that of crystalline sulfur to polished gold. Adrian went to that one first in order to make a more careful study, followed meekly by Meryl, while Angelica hung back, watching them—or, to be more specific, watching Adrian.

"You'll have to give me a running commentary," Meryl said to Adrian. "I'll do my damnedest to see what I can, but I'll definitely need help."

Adrian did his best to oblige, uncomfortably aware that the artist was listening, and doubtless poised to pick up any error of vision or inference.

The study in sulfur and gold was, not at all to his surprise, a picture of the mythical Golden Fleece, with a triumphant Jason displaying it to an invisible crowd. Medea was not present—unless she was invisible, although that would probably have been taking subtlety too far. The Jason in the picture wasn't exactly a portrait, but it was obvious to Adrian that he was clearly based on Angelica's husband: a younger and more muscular version than the one they had left behind in the dining room.

It was a pity, Adrian thought, although he did not express the thought aloud, that the image of Jason in the painting was invisible to the real Jason, who would doubtless have thought it a compliment. He did not think that the real Jason could pick up any impression of his presence within the splodge subliminally. In explaining the picture to Meryl, he merely described the subject, and offered no esthetic judgment. Nor did she, being equally aware of Angelica's presence and wary of offending her. Had Jason Jarndyke been present, Adrian knew, he would not only have been far more voluble but overtly inquisitive—which was, he presumed, why Angelica had deliberately excluded him from the showing.

The study in yellow reassured him somewhat, after the anxieties he'd built up in consequence of the Dantean image of the inferno. It was, all things considered, a pleasant enough picture, which seemed to have been painted with a degree of affection. Angelica had obviously known that her husband would not be able to see the image suggestive of himself, but she had not been tempted to be satirical in the depiction, let alone cruel. There was no mockery in it. In fact, it made its young Jason look like a true hero, a genuine Argonaut—as, of course, the real Jason was, in his own field and his own more mature fashion.

The study in blue was a mermaid, or perhaps a siren—Adrian had never been clear in his mind as to whether or not they were the same thing. She was not, however, a Hans Christian Andersen mermaid: a meek self-sacrificing innocent who had consented to walk

136

on daggers for a lifetime in exchange for the privilege of being able to keep a fisherman company. On the other hand, nor did she give the impression of being a malevolent *femme fatale*: a temptress, able and eager to lead men to their doom with a seductive song.

"Is it a self-portrait?" Meryl immediately asked, presumably wondering whether it was a counterpart to the Jason.

The question put Adrian into a slight quandary. Chronologically, he was sure, it was the second picture in the set, and the limitations of Angelica's draughtsmanship, more obvious in the top half of the central figure than the bottom, might have been responsible for the difficulty of seeing any resemblance to Angelica in the mermaid's face, but he came to a decision quickly enough.

"No, it's not," he said. "It's a purely hypothetical mermaid, an incarnation of an idea rather than a transfiguration of a person."

And in that regard, he thought, the chimera was intriguing. The fishy part was sharply delineated, elegantly curled and beautifully colored in the scales, which were silvery within all the myriad blue reflections of water-modified sky. The human half, by contrast, was not only deliberately vague, but the rippling blue hair seemed in need of the attentions of a good hairdresser, and the features were rather flat, the expression resigned rather than alluring. Again, Adrian limited himself to a description of the theme in explaining it to Meryl, without any comment on the execution, or the possible symbolism.

But might it be a sort of portrait, in spite of the absence of any obvious physical resemblance in the features? Adrian wondered, privately. Might the siren be a means by which Angelica was trying to represent her inner rather than her outer self? If so, what did the distinction between the piscine and human parts, and the blankness of the expression signify? Loneliness, perhaps . . . a sense of difference, probably . . . but what else?

Adrian had always felt more comfortable in confrontation with pure exercises in color and form, like Rothko's or Pollock's. Monet's gardens, too, he felt that he understood very well, and Georgia O'Keefe's flowers. But with regard to Dante Gabriel Rossetti, his sentiments had been more mixed; he had appreciated the pre-Raphaelite attention to detail, but had been disconcerted by the quality of his women's faces, and the extreme subtleties of attitude they presumably reflected, toward the models with which he had had such tortured and convoluted personal relationships. Adrian was well aware, though, that that disconcertion might say more about himself than the painter.

Unsurprisingly, Adrian found the blue siren far less unsettling than the red inferno, but there was still a primitive hint of damnation in the picture that seemed menacing as well as uncanny—a hint that became more pronounced as the sequence went on.

The study in green was an image of forest foliage, with hidden faces peeping slyly through it: nymphs of various sorts and fauns, seemingly all similar, although some of the faces were too vague to be identifiable, even by species, let alone as individuals. Some tended to the ugly, some to the beautiful, but none to the meek and sanitized. On the other hand, they were not exactly malevolent either—merely somewhat unhuman, weirdly hybridized. The description he gave Meryl was suitably vague.

The composition of the picture, and the manner in which the foliage and the faces were intermingled, was very ambitious—perhaps a trifle too ambitious, although it showed off the artist's evolving and increasingly confident technique to better effect than the simpler and more straightforward images. Complication helped to offset a few slight individual faults of curvature. It was easier to see in this picture that Angelica had had some professional training, and had benefited from it, in spite of being handicapped by inexperience, and as-yet-insufficient skill in her brushwork.

It must, Adrian thought, have become apparent to her during the slightly less than two years she had spent at the Courtauld before leaving to concentrate on her modeling career, that she might never be able to create a work of art as wonderful as the one she constituted in herself, even with the aid of full-spectrum color vision. She had not given up, though. She had carried on painting in private, with considerable determination and intensity—albeit concentrating increasingly on work that only she could see.

The study in pale brown was sand: Egyptian sand, to judge by the ruins and statuary projecting through it at intervals. Some of the half-buried statues had faces, but they were not really human faces; Adrian felt sure that they were the faces of sphinxes, and communicated that impression to Meryl. He even quoted Shelley's immortal line—"Look on my works, ye mighty, and despair!"—as if it were the theme of the picture, but Ozymandias was not there, and he rapidly amended his verdict to say that the quotation did not really sum up the tenor of the picture. He risked an explanatory critical evaluation: "It's not celebrating or regretting the decay that has all-but-erased the residue of a once-great civilization, but using the extreme subtlety of color to imply a near-identity between the stones and the sand, the shaped and the shapeless."

Meryl looked at him skeptically, as if to say: *What is that even supposed to mean?* but she let it pass without oral comment.

What *is* it supposed to mean, though? Adrian wondered, groping for the impression he had been trying ineptly to formulate. The desert scene was certainly an austere picture, an image of aridity, and probably reflected a sense of existential aridity, an image of what Horst Koerner had called "innate melancholy." Adrian did not know what to make of the peeping, broken sphinxes, gradually fading into dust in the wake of their makers.

The study in dark brown, on the other hand, was a calculated exercise in the sinister and the supernatural, which seemed to be aiming far more consciously and deliberately to create a sense of unease by concealing its effects just out of the range of ordinary human sight. That one, Adrian thought might not have seemed like a mere splodge even to Jason Jarndyke, although Meryl was hard-pressed to identify anything in it other than tree-trunks and branches when she volunteered to try. It was another forest, but not a leafy forest—there were only a few hints of dark green in the mix. This was a dense forest seen from within, all gnarled tree-trunks and decaying humus. This forest was inhabited, as the other had been, but not by conventional mythological creatures. There were strange squirrels and squatting toads, whose air of menace was not contained in anything as obvious as fangs and claws, but in a peculiar implication of *disease*.

It was a deliberately ugly painting, and Adrian wondered whether Angelica might simply have thought it easier to paint the ugly than the beautiful, given her awareness of her persistent technical limitations, and had simply decided, in this instance, to play to her strengths. He was reluctant to jump too readily to the conclusion that there might be any deep psychological significance in it, because it seemed too obviously contrived, in order to be horrid. For that reason, he found it slightly amusing, like an ancient schlock-horror movie striving a little too hard for effect—but it was the first picture in the series in which it seemed to him that Angelica was deliberately trying to produce something capable of affecting its viewers subliminally, capable of communicating a sense of nastiness and threat to people would could only obtain the vaguest impression of what it might be intended to represent. It was the first picture in the chronological sequence that appeared to be attempting a sort of artistic witchcraft.

The two studies in black—the most recent pictures of the seven, if his estimate could be trusted—were where the actual witches figured, however. In one, they were stereotypical witches in black conical hats, gathered around a cauldron. It was like a scene from *Macbeth*, and might well have been exactly that. It was redolent with dramatic tradition—a tradition that did not seem, in this representation, to have been excessively tarnished by the travesties of Hallowe'en. Adrian felt slightly embarrassed describing it for Meryl, knowing that Angelica was listening to his account, and knowing that she would doubtless have heard unkind remarks about her own supposed penchant for witchcraft, but Meryl was careful not to wonder aloud whether there was any suggestion of self-portraiture about it.

The other black canvas was quite different in its subtle shades; in that one there was a black tower, and black cats, and a black-clad witch standing tall and imperious at the summit, evidently the mistress of all she surveyed. Most of the servile witches gathered around the cauldron down below were hagwives, but one of them, standing in front of the tower, accompanied by an unnaturally large cat, was more akin to the Arthurian Morgan le Fay, a custodian of the kind of cold, implacable beauty that Medusa might have had before her hair became snaky and her gaze literally lethal. Her stare was not murderous, in any straightforward sense, but it was definitely malevolent. She seemed to be an officer in the Witch Empress' army of evildoers.

As he gave Meryl the barest verbal sketch of the image, Adrian could hardly help returning, in the course of his own preoccupation, to the question of whether the dark Fay was a kind of self-portrait, a dream of some dark doppelgänger, but again he rejected the hypothesis, at least in any simple sense.

Neither of the studies in black was a calculated attempt to produce something subliminally frightening, as the second forest scene seemed to be. To some extent, they were purely technical experiments in the deployment of the subtle shades that the common eye lumped together as "black," their common theme chosen as a matter of ready-made propriety—ready-made, at any rate, for someone who did not immediately associate black, as Adrian did, with modern technologies of artificial photosynthesis. Given that the latter was the connection that free association brought automatically to his mind, though, it was easy for him to imagine the darkness in the pictures soaking up the sun's energy, in order to generate . . . what? Perhaps pure magic; raw power of a different sort.

"I don't really like them," Meryl admitted, frankly, of the studies in black, with an anxious sideways glance at Angelica. "There's something discomfiting about them. Is it just the psychological effect of the color black, do you think, or do pictures of witches retain a subliminal power of disturbance that distinct images have lost, devalued by overuse?"

"That's possible," Adrian conceded. "Quite likely, in fact. Visual images do become devalued, as familiarity breeds contempt, while liminal perception, which retains an essential uncertainty and ambiguity, allows them to remain disturbing."

Meryl turned to Angelica. "And that's what you're actually trying to do, isn't it? That's the effect you're aiming for . . . and the one you showed us last week is the most successful one you've produced to date. You've actually been working up, gradually, to producing what looks to ordinary eyes to be abstract, but which the unconscious mind perceives as scary?"

"That's a perceptive summation, my dear," said Angelica, in an oddly atonal voice. "You obviously have the appreciative eye that advancement in your profession cultivates and requires." She did not even glance at Meryl while she spoke, though. Her gaze was still riveted to Adrian, searching for his reaction—but he was not yet ready to let it show.

"Well, I'm sorry, Mrs. Jarndyke," Meryl continued, "but I have to confess that I prefer the brighter ones. Perhaps I'm just shallow, but I like the yellow one best. I can appreciate the technical artistry of what you're doing in the darker images, now I have a better idea of why the studies in black and red make me feel slightly queasy, but . . . well, I'd rather get a sense of the beautiful out of a picture than a sense of the sublime."

"That's because you're happy," Angelica commented. "At least for the moment."

Meryl flinched slightly, but swallowed the retort that undoubtedly sprang to her lips. She was a guest in Angelica's house, after all. Adrian thought that he ought to intervene, even though he still had not made up his mind what he really thought of the strange exhibition.

"It's brilliant work," he said. "All of it, although your technique and your artistry have made a lot of progress since the yellow and the blue—and I think it shows a keen insight into the psychology of the exercise to have gone on from the studies in black to the red inferno. It's thoroughly sensible, I think, to have started with exercises intended for the subliminal stimulation of unease, because that's far more fundamental within the emotional spectrum than the more positive and delicate emotions. I'd be very interested to see how you've progressed from the Inferno . . . whether you've tried to go further in the same direction, or whether you've aimed for something . . . more positive."

It was very difficult to tell, given the solidity of her mask, but Adrian got the impression that Angelica was slightly disappointed by that. She had no right to be, he thought. What had she been expecting, after all?

"I'm not ready to show my more recent work yet," she said. "It's not finished . . . and I'm beginning to wonder whether it's worth finishing. Perhaps I'd be wise to seek your advice about that, Adrian, given that you've given me such extensive proof that you can see exactly what I'm doing, and can understand it—even if, like Meryl, you don't really approve. But I think I need to know you a little better first."

"I don't disapprove," Adrian said. "I'm a scientist. I understand the spirit of experimentation, and its difficulties. I appreciate and admire the progress that you've made, and the potential you still have. The possibilities are literally endless, and you're a genuine pioneer. You have every reason to be extremely proud of what you've done—and of being able to see what amazing things still remain to be attempted."

This time the impassivity cracked. In theory, Adrian supposed, she might have smiled at the compliment, but he knew her well enough by now to anticipate that her reaction would be quite different. She didn't quite scowl, but for a second or two, she reacted exactly as if his remark had been a deadly insult. Then, however, if he read her correctly, she realized that she had made an error, that Adrian really had not meant any harm, that the inference she had taken was in error. He would have liked to emphasize that fact, to try to reassure her that he really was on her side, but he didn't know how, and thought that any attempt he might make would sound stupid.

"Thank you, Adrian," Angelica said, having recovered her composure. "I appreciate the vote of confidence, although I don't really deserve it. You're not disappointed by the pictures, then? I got the impression, while you were looking at them, that you were searching for something you didn't find."

And there it is, Adrian thought. *The truth.*

She knew that he had been searching the paintings for a representation of an elusive shadow. Ergo, she could see them too. But did their absence mean that she could not see them clearly enough to depict them, or because she was afraid to do so? Had Meryl not been present, he might have asked her the question directly, and entered into the dialogue that she must be as anxious to have as he was—but it was not a discussion that he wanted to have in front of a third party, and he was uncomfortably aware of the fact that Jason Jarndyke must be waiting with extreme impatience to be allowed back into their colloquium.

146

"You're right, Mrs. Jarndyke," he said, "but that flaw is in me, not in your paintings. I was looking for something more, but I should have known better. It's necessary, as well as sensible, to do the simpler things first and build up to the more complicated ones. As your husband would say, the kind of enterprise you're undertaking is a marathon, not a sprint."

She tried to smile at that, and might have succeeded on a better day.

"And he would inevitably have added that Rome wasn't built in a day . . . and that they botched the job anyway," she agreed.

"I don't get it," Meryl put in. "What were you looking for that isn't there, even invisibly?"

Adrian hesitated, not knowing what to reply. Angelica stepped in.

"It's difficult to explain," she said. "Don't give Adrian a hard time about it, Meryl—it's something that we don't understand. Perhaps we will, in time, with a little help from one another, but for the moment . . . well, it probably has much the same effect on us as the paintings have on you: it makes us uneasy, without our being able to say exactly why. No matter how much enhanced vision allows a person to see, the darkness beyond is always infinite, and at the limit of vision there are still . . ." She stopped, not knowing how to express it.

"Elusive shadows," Adrian supplied.

"Yes, exactly," Angelica agreed. "Except, of course, *exact* is exactly what they're not. As for the paintings, I can understand why you don't like them . . . in fact, as you say, there's a sense in which that's the effect that they were suppose to have. Perhaps that's perverse, but Adrian's right when he says that it makes sense to start by generating the simplest responses first. I wanted to *do* something, you see. I wanted to see whether I could have an effect . . . *any* effect. You can understand that, can't you?"

Successfully, and artfully, steered away from the issue of the elusive shadows, Meryl nodded her head. "Yes, I can," she admitted. "I know the feeling well enough."

"The point is," Adrian said, addressing Meryl, while waving his arm to take in the seven paintings, "that this is amazing work. Nobody else in the world could have done this. Nobody else in the world could have shown us this, and we both ought to be truly grateful to Mrs. Jarndyke for letting us see it."

"But I can't see it," Meryl pointed out. "Which is the whole point of the exercise, isn't it? Nobody can see it—except you."

"Not just me. Somewhere, there must be others. And in future . . . sight evolves, under pressure of natural selection, coupled with the desire to see. Perhaps people like you need paintings like this, to function as a spur, or a lure, a suggestion of possibilities that you might attain, if only you can develop and train neural pathways that might already exist, in a dormant or latent form. Perhaps we don't have as much potential as bees, with their versatile compound eyes and their highly-developed color sensitivity, because we haven't had the same selective pressures operating on us, but even if we don't, we're entering the age of sophisticated genetic engineering now, and we're beginning to understand the physiological bases of vision. In time, if they want to, our descendants will be able to see far better than we can—Mrs. Jarndyke and I are merely a hint of posthumanity to come."

"*Bees?*" Meryl repeated, incredulously. "You think bees can see more than we can?"

"Absolutely," said Adrian. "Hummingbirds too. There's a wider range of pigmentation in nature—and hence a wider range of pigment-producing genes—than the average human eye can discriminate. Natural selection produced them; ergo there must be organisms that can see them—the organisms to which the colors are, so to speak, addressed. Pollinators that the flowers are competing to attract with the aid of beautiful flowers: bees, hummingbirds and dozens of other species."

Meryl and Angelica both nodded, in a particular fashion, to confirm that they could follow the argument.

"Perhaps, one day," Adrian went on, "when everyone is able to see as Mrs. Jarndyke and I can see, her paintings will be hanging in every gallery and museum on Earth, revered as the pioneering foundation stones of a whole new dimension of artistic endeavor. Other artists might do better, in time, but Angelica Jarndyke will always have been the first, and Mr. Jarndyke, you and I, Meryl, will always have been the first to see them. That really is quite a privilege, and we ought to appreciate it for its full worth."

"Unless, of course," Angelica put in, "somewhere, lying neglected in some dusty attic or the storerooms of some lunatic asylum, painted by some other poor wife whose husband didn't know anything about art, but knew what he didn't like . . ."

"With all due respect, Mrs. Jarndyke," Adrian said, not interrupting her, because she had deliberately trailed off for theatrical effect, leaving it to her listeners, "don't you think that you're being a little unkind to your husband? He brought me here because he believed that you'd be happy to find someone who actually could see your work—and he wanted to please you, to have someone you could actually believe tell you that your work is good. I think I can understand why you're not as glad as he hoped, but I'm sure that he can't. If . . ."

She did interrupt. "You want me to pretend to be over the moon?" she snapped. "For your sake?"

"It's not for me to ask you to do anything, Mrs. Jarndyke—but if I did want you to pretend, it would be for his sake, not mine. He's not at fault. He might not give a damn about Rothko or Emmanuel Vigelund, but he really would like to be able to appreciate your painting. It worries him that he can't—but it isn't his fault."

Adrian almost continued, but decided that he might already have said too much. Jason Jarndyke was his employer, and he had to make every possible effort not to cause any difficulty. He took a step toward the door, hoping that the three of them could simply go back to the dining room, where he could tell Jason Jarndyke once again what a magnificent artist his wife was, and how grateful he was to have seen her work.

Angelica wouldn't let him. She didn't do anything as crude as blocking his way, but she stopped him in his tracks with a glance. Beautiful women could do that, Adrian knew, even when a man had a lover with whom he was contentedly besotted standing right beside him. He couldn't help a slight superstitious shudder.

"Why?" she said. "You think you understand—so why am I not glad?"

Adrian thought about it, and decided to opt for diplomacy: "Perhaps I'm over-reaching my competence, Mrs. Jarndyke, in claiming that I understand. But I do know that there's been a misunderstanding—that your reaction to discovering that I can see your paintings wasn't at all what your husband expected, and still isn't. I know that, in a sense, I've let him down. He wanted to make you a gift of my eyes, of my special sight, because he thinks that you've been yearning for an audience for all the fifteen years that you've been married, and maybe longer. In fact, he's only succeeded in distressing you, and I don't want that any more than he does. Can we go back, now, please? You have no use for me here; it was very kind of you to let me see your paintings, and I'm truly grateful for it, but I'd like to return to your husband now, for the sake of politeness."

He had been trying to smooth things over, to worm his way out of his predicament, but he could see in Angelica Jarndyke's marvelously beautiful face that he'd only made things worse. He cursed himself for having been a fool, for not having known what to say and for not having had the sense simply to keep quiet.

"What would *you* have done?" she asked, in a deadly whisper.

That, Adrian realized, was what she really wanted to know. She was only a Yorkshirewoman by marriage, he knew, but he didn't think she'd have much patience if he simply continued beating around the bush, so he stopped.

"I've asked myself that, once or twice, since I saw your *Inferno*," he admitted. "What would I have done if, as well as being able to see the full color spectrum, and teach myself to identify and analyze a significant fraction of its psychological effects, I'd also been able to paint? For a little while, it seemed like a conundrum, but then I realized that I already had the answer. I'd have done something analogous to what I am doing, with my own particular talent. Instead of studying genetics, in order to generate as many of the spectrum's gradations of color in different organic pigments, I'd have done what you did, and gone to art school to learn technique. And when I'd learned the tricks of the trade, I'd have looked for an opportunity to apply them—but I'd have looked for a way to apply them in such a way that people could see what I was doing, perhaps not entirely consciously, but nevertheless visibly.

"I'd have done what other painters with your particular talent have done in the past, using all the colors of the palette in individual paintings. I'd have painted images that even people like Mr. Jarndyce could see without effort: portraits, flowers, foliage . . . maybe even sirens, fauns and witches. I'd have used my additional powers of discrimination to build in extra levels of suggestion, tantalizingly beyond the easy reach of commonplace consciousness, but I wouldn't have tried to hide what I was representing; I wouldn't have created an entire occult art that, so far as I knew, *nobody* else would ever be able to see . . . something for myself alone. Maybe that makes me less than a true artist. Maybe it makes me into a commercial hack, just looking for a way to market my talent. But that's what I do—and that's what I would have done, if I'd been able to paint but had no aptitude for science. I suppose I'd have gone into advertising."

Adrian was afraid that Angelica Jarndyke might take offense at the implicit criticism, and that she might be fully entitled to do so—but if her sentiments inclined her in that direction, she controlled them. She didn't go so far as to nod her head to concede the justice of his case, but she didn't oppose it.

"I suppose you'd like to see the barn now," she said, mildly. If it was a question at all, it was a hypothetical one. Adrian knew that it wasn't an offer.

"No, thank you," he said.

He knew that it was a mistake as soon as the words were out of his mouth. He realized immediately that he should have said "Yes please!" as eagerly as possible. That way, she could have asserted herself by refusing. As things stood now, he'd issued a tacit challenge.

"Liar," she said.

"Honesty doesn't come into it," he lied, clumsily. "I don't think it would be a good idea for me to look at your recent work, given that this isn't working out the way that Mr. Jarndyke hoped it would. There's nothing

I can do for him here. It would certainly be interesting to see your work . . . but I will confess, having seen your studies in black and red, that I'm a little afraid of the effect it might have on me."

"Coward, then," she amended.

"Very much so," Adrian admitted. "May we please go back to Mr. Jarndyke now?"

It was her turn to lie. "Nobody's stopping you," she said, and raised her arm as if to show him the way, in case he'd forgotten where the door was.

All three of them went back to the dining room, and Adrian spent a dutiful twenty minutes telling Jason Jarndyke what a magnificent painter his wife was, and what a privilege it had been to see her works, while Meryl, while not exactly sulking, made no attempt to hide her bewilderment at what had just happened, and her annoyance at not having been able to understand.

Angelica Jarndyke made no attempt to challenge Adrian's praise, having reverted to a policy of not looking at anyone, and only making the most blatantly tokenistic efforts to take part in the conversation. Her husband did not seem offended by that, or even disappointed, in spite of the snub that had left him in the dining room while his wife had shown her pictures to his guests. His optimism was still intact. He still seemed to imagine that she was "coming round," and that she would soon be duly grateful to him for discovering Adrian, and making her a gift of his miraculous sight.

Jason Jarndyke had no more idea than Meryl as to what was really going on in his wife's mind, Adrian thought. How could he, given that he was more than averagely unsighted, even though he was convinced that he could see with perfectly clarity, and was honest enough to call a splodge a splodge?

Meryl, perhaps wisely, said almost nothing more as the afternoon wound down—but Adrian knew that she would interrogate him at length later, and that she would probably keep on interrogating him until he had told her what on earth was going on between the Jarndykes, and between him and Angelica, or until their own relationship came to an acrimonious end— which was the last thing he wanted.

Unfortunately, even though he thought that he did have at least the beginnings of an understanding of Angelica's psychology, he was not yet in a position to explain that hypothesis to Meryl, any more than he had been ready to explain it to Angelica. He needed to know more. First of all, and most essentially, he needed to know whether Angelica could see the elusive shadows any more clearly than he could, and, in any case, what she thought they might be.

11

There was no question, this time, of waiting for Jayjay to drop by his desk or his lab with another invitation to the Old Manse. The game had gone beyond that. Adrian was expecting a direct approach, and it was a great relief when he found that he didn't have to remain in suspense for days on end.

Whether Jason Jardyke, and therefore Angelica, had some way of knowing whether he was at home, and whether he was alone there, or whether it was pure coincidence that Meryl was busy at a function at Salt's Mill on the Monday while Adrian was spending the evening in the apartment catching up on his reading, he had no idea. Nevertheless, it was when there was no prospect of their being disturbed for several hours that the doorbell of the apartment rang, at quarter to eight in the evening. He guessed immediately who it would be, but he feigned astonishment anyway. He invited Angelica Jarndyke in, and offered her a cup of coffee, which she accepted once he had confirmed that he had no alcohol to hand.

She was still wearing her mask, after a fashion. Once she had taken off the capacious dark blue hooded cape in which she had slipped down the hill from the Old Manse and up two flights of stairs in the apartment block, she was clad with meticulous elegance and had applied her make-up with skill and neatness, but her expression was more than a trifle distraught and anxious. Not only had she still not fully recovered from the bout of depression that had set in after his first visit to the Manse, Adrian thought, but she had suffered a slight relapse since the previous day, perhaps unsurprisingly.

Adoptive Yorkshirewoman or not, she began by beating around the bush. "I'm truly sorry about the way I behaved yesterday, Adrian." she said. "I haven't been quite myself lately."

"I fear that's my fault," Adrian said, not merely as a polite gesture. "Obviously, your husband had told you about me beforehand, but having the claim confirmed and realizing that someone—not just someone, but some puny youth your husband had hired straight out of university to color his biotech fabrics—could actually see your paintings, after all this time . . . it must have been a shock."

"It was," she agreed, "but that doesn't make you responsible. I've had bouts like this before. Doctors of various stripes have confirmed that I'm not bipolar, but haven't been able to come up with anything that even sounds like a plausible diagnosis. Not surprising, really, as I appear to be a highly idiosyncratic case—but not quite unique, it seems. Do you . . . ?" She didn't spell it out, but it was obvious that she was asking whether he had bouts of deep depression too, perhaps hoping that it was simply a side-effect of her enhanced vision.

"Not in the same way." he said. "I do understand the feelings, honestly . . . the isolation, the frustration, having to doubt one's own sanity . . . but as soon as I began to understand them, I knew that I needed to develop ways of containing them. Mostly, I fought the tendency to depression with calculated obsession—which has a certain neatness, I suppose. I also, without exactly meaning to, suppressed my ability to feel anything. I represent it to myself as being rational and disciplined, but really it's just a kind of mental anesthetization. I hadn't realized how far it had gone until . . ." He stopped.

"Until you met Meryl," she said, dryly. "I suppose that irritated me yesterday, too, although that really does reflect badly on me. To be unhappy oneself is one thing, but to react badly to seeing other people happy . . . well, I hadn't realized how far *that* had gone, until yesterday. Jason's delighted, of course, not just because it's the first time one of his clumsy attempted fix-ups actually seems to have worked, but because he thinks you being such a 'fast worker,' as he puts it, is an extra facet of your genius. It wasn't in your CV, apparently, or the report that his headhunting agency complied on you."

"It wouldn't be," Adrian admitted, wryly. "And it still isn't. I didn't do anything at all. The work, if it was work—and I still have a nagging suspicion that it might have been—was all Meryl's. As the cliché has it, she swept me off my feet, almost literally. I owe her a great debt of gratitude, although it has left me somewhat off balance. So, like you, I don't feel that I'm quite myself at present, either."

Angelica contrived a half-smile at that. "Maybe," she said. "But cliché-wise, you're over the moon and I'm down in the dumps. I envy you—not so much because of that, as because of the rest: the rationality and the discipline. I've tried to fight it with obsession too, believe me, but without much success. And although I do have the love of a good man and a stable anchorage, it's never . . . well, let's just say that I hope your relationship with Meryl works out, and gives you everything you need in that regard."

Adrian managed not to wince, but couldn't help thinking that the odds against that were probably a million to one, even if sweeping him off his feet turned out not to have been merely a tactical move on Meryl's part and that she really did have the capacity to become genuinely fond of him.

Angelica seemed to read the thought. "Not confident, eh? Well, that's not just you and me—that's everyone. Nobody ever knows for sure. I don't suppose it's any easier for a shy and callow intellectual starting his first real job than it is for a trophy wife with neuroses and a surface that's beginning to tarnish, but . . . well, Jason deserves better. He's a good man. He thinks I'm in the barn, by the way . . . I don't need to ask you, do I, to keep this confidential?"

"We're not actually doing anything wrong, Mrs. Jarndyke," Adrian pointed out. "We've been properly introduced, and we have interests in common . . . perfectly innocent things in common. Would Mr. Jarndyke really mind if he knew that we wanted to discuss those common interests, in private?"

"Rationally, no," Angelica admitted—without, Adrian noted, inviting him to call her Angelica rather than Mrs. Jarndyke—"but it's not as simple as that. He has his neuroses too, feelings he can't help. It's not that his bonhomie is faked—he really is a good man, a nice man—but he's also a trifle brittle. Not that I should be using his potential jealousy as an excuse, when I'm the one who has the urge to hide, to keep this a deep, dark secret. You can understand why, can't you?"

Her gaze abruptly took on the sharp intensity that was now becoming almost familiar. Apparently, the bush was now thoroughly beaten, and it was time to get to the nub of the matter. After all, they didn't have all night.

"Yes, I can," he said quietly—but he was still sufficiently intimidated to hesitate momentarily over voicing the real issue.

She wasn't quite ready to cut directly to the quick herself, and there were other questions she wanted, and probably needed, to ask. He watched her toy with her coffee cup for a few moments, shifting uneasily in her armchair.

"Have you met any others?" she asked, in a slightly subdued voice

"Others with better than average color perception, certainly," he said, "but no one as adept as me—or you."

"You seem to be much better at detecting others than I am," she said. "I had suspicions about certain artists, but I never felt sure, the way you seem to be."

"I might overreach the actual warrant of the evidence sometimes—almost certainly, in fact," Adrian admitted. "That's one of the more treacherous aspects of the scientific mind. But it's helped me a lot to have the scientific method at my disposal, not only for enabling me to look for evidence in the abilities of others of enhanced perceptions similar to mine, but more importantly still, to enable me to try to understand myself, to organize myself and discipline myself. As soon as I had a theoretical framework in which to set the ability, as one phenomenon among many, only unique in myself to a matter of degree, I had a way of dealing with it. Detecting it, especially in artists, became a game . . . or another aspect of my obsession."

"I didn't have that," she said. "I could only think of it as magic . . . one of those seeming gifts that turns out to be more of a curse, like the Midas touch: the real evil eye, in fact. If I tried to reach an understanding by study, it was in that context. I suppose you've heard that I'm a witch?"

"The word has been mentioned," Adrian confirmed. "I don't take it seriously."

"Nobody does. Everybody says it in jest. Watch out for Medea, ha ha. Only it's not entirely a joke . . . and I understand that perfectly, because it's not entirely a joke to me either. There have been times . . . perhaps all the time . . . when I really do feel like a witch, a servant of Hecate, or even Satan. You read that, didn't you? You might not think much of my technique, but you know that it was no accident that I showed you the study in scarlet first, hiding the flames of Hell. I watched you looking at the rest too, and the studies in black. I knew exactly what you were looking for. I saw the frustration when you didn't find it . . . and that, not the week before, was when I knew for sure that you really were like me . . . not that it excuses my being so rude. But I think you do understand why that not only doesn't delight me, the way poor Jason thought it would, and still thinks it ought to, but why it actually hurts?"

Softly, Adrian said: "For what its worth, Mrs. Jarndyke, I really am very glad indeed to have met you, and I'm truly sorry that you don't feel the same way."

"So am I," she said. "And you have no idea how much I wish that Jason's right, and that I'll come round eventually. But it's not that easy, you see. Not for a witch. Envy of your scientific detachment makes it even worse, because it makes me feel like an utter failure. If only I could have been like you . . . if only I could become . . . but the hell with that. I could never have got away with it. You look the part. I don't. People have expectations of women who look like me. We're not living in the twentieth century any more, when it was simply assumed that pretty women had to be stupid, but image still counts. You can get away with being analytical, pretentious and pedantic, Dr. Stamford, and still have pretty things like Meryl falling over themselves to fuck you, it seems, but it doesn't exactly befit a *femme fatale* whose destined career, whether it's her ambition or not, is to be a trophy wife. I was stereotyped as a witch by the great casting director in the sky long before I convinced myself that I was one—in jest, of course, but not entirely. No offense intended, by the way."

162

"None taken," Adrian assured her, not insincerely. "I do try not to be pretentious, but the scientific turn of mind keeps coming through. People call it pedantic, but it's not really." Only a pedant, he knew, would pull people up on the propriety of their use of the term "pedantic," but he didn't voice the joke. It was hardly the time.

"If I'd only been able to see things the way you see them, I'd probably have gone into advertising, as you said you might have done if you could practice art as well as think about it. Witches and *femmes fatales* can do that . . . hell, even bimbos can do that. What a marriage I might have had then, eh? Jason and I could be partners instead of strangers . . . not that it would be any guarantee of happiness. In fact, it would probably have been a short cut to the divorce court. Sorry—you must think I'm an ungrateful bitch. Nine women out of ten would kill for my looks, and I just resent the way they define me. I have everything I need to be happy—devoted husband, nice kids, more money than Croesus—but I just can't do it. The fault isn't in my stars but in me . . . and *them*."

The intensity, having faded away temporarily, was back. Impatient with her own dithering, she had taken the fatal plunge. And Adrian could tell, even though her composure was magnificent, that she was terrified.

"The elusive shadows," he said, quietly.

"That's a good name," she said. "I even envy you that. I was stupid enough, or crazy enough, to pull terms out of a different vocabulary, not even in jest. Ghosts, demons . . . but mostly just *them*. Not a neutral *them*: a *them* loaded with menace, always ominous. I've told myself a million times that there isn't the slightest shred of evidence that they're dangerous or hostile, but it's like telling yourself that spiders are utterly innocuous. It's fine until you see a big one crawling across the carpet, and then you shudder and jump on to the table. And I've told myself a million times, too, that they aren't even real, that they're just a kind of optical illusion, or a glitch in my mentality. And that was fine, too . . . until Jason introduced me to you, and made me put you to the test, and suddenly, the possibility was there that if you could see them too, then they really were real, and out there . . . and ominous. Anyway, as you obviously know full well, that's why I'm here. I'm scared to death of what you might tell me, but I do need to know. You can see them too. Two is the magic number. They really are out there. But what the fuck are they? Can you tell me that, *Doctor* Stamford?"

There was no point in dishonesty. "No, I can't," he said. "I've formed hypotheses, obviously—that's what I do, after all. I've even lingered momentarily over the hypotheses that immediately occurred to you, because of the direction of your approach: the idea that they might be the shades of the dead, or even demons . . . or, at the very least, that their existence might help to account for the legendry of ghosts and demons. Not unnaturally, I prefer hypotheses of a different sort, more plausible within my way of thinking. But no—I don't know what they are, and I can't put your mind at rest immediately. But one of the reasons why I'm glad to know that your perception is as highly-developed as mine, is that I hope that, by pooling our observations, we might be better placed to draw conclusions than either of us was when we were confronting the problem on our own."

"Two heads being better than one?" she queried, her expression now unreadable.

"Yes—and not in a simple numerical sense. I'm hoping that the different talents with which we support and elaborate our perceptions might allow our contributions to be complementary. Perhaps that's optimistic, but after Meryl, I can't help . . ."

"What do you mean, *after Meryl?*" she interrupted.

"She can't see."

"No, but as an example of complementarity, it's not irrelevant. She insists that sleeping with me isn't a *quid pro quo* for my agreeing to collaborate with her, to provide her with fuel for her publications record, but I'm not sure I can believe her. She spotted immediately, the day before, when we were chatting about art over dinner, that my insights could be extremely useful to her, precisely because they were looking at things from a viewpoint different from hers, and I think she decided then that it was worth making an effort to seduce me. I suspect that she thinks that if she weren't having sex with me, she'd simply be exploiting me for her own ends—but in fact, she wouldn't, because the contribution she can bring to the interpretation and elaboration of my perceptions is by no means trivial. And even though the cases aren't similar, that realization boosted my hope that combining your perception of the elusive shadows with mine might, at the very least, help to favor one of the many hypotheses I've entertained over the others."

For a moment, Adrian was afraid that Angelica would get hold of the wrong end of the stick and tell him, firmly, that she had no intention of having sex with him, but she was too intelligent for that. She got the real point of the argument and the analogy.

"You think that, although we're both seeing the same thing, we might be seeing it slightly differently? That if we combine our impressions, we might get a clearer picture than either one of us has been able to obtain alone?"

"Exactly."

She didn't seem as hopeful as he had hoped. "I'm not sure I'm going to be any use to you," she said. "They're essentially frustrating—things I glimpse out of the corner of my eye, but which disappear as soon as I try to look at them directly. For me, they're always peripheral. Elusive shadows, as you say. They modify the color of whatever they're gliding over, but they don't seem to have any color of their own. As for shape and structure, I only have the vaguest impression . . . I really can't . . . *are* they shadows, do you think? Shadows of *something else*?"

"That's one of the hypotheses I've been considering," Adrian admitted, "although it introduced certain conceptual difficulties. But you mustn't sell yourself short. You might have seen more than you think. Can we start with the basics. I'll begin, and you can say yea or nay, and then you can add your impressions, so that I can confirm or deny that my experience tallies. Okay?"

166

"Go on."

"Right. First of all, they seem to vary in size between a cricket ball and a basketball, although they're not circular, or oval, and their irregularity varies. Their edges aren't sharp, but blurred. Does that tally with your impressions?"

"Yes."

"They're rarely seen indoors, although they're capable of coming inside, and they're much more common at night than in daylight. It's rare to see more than one at a time, but at night there are sometimes two, or even three, simultaneously in view. Right?"

"True."

"Your turn: tell me how they move."

"They don't, usually, but they can. If they do, well, they seem to me to *flow*. Maybe they float, but they give me the impression of a pool of liquid moving over the surface of things rather than gliding through the air. They sometimes move very fast, disappearing almost instantly . . . and sometimes, they do seem actually to disappear . . . especially if you look at them directly. That's what made me decide, in the end, that they had to be some kind of optical illusion, not something real . . . although, given that you can see them too, I suppose . . ."

"Let's not get ahead of ourselves. What about internal structure?"

"That's difficult, especially because they disappear when I try to focus on them, but I get the impression that they're . . . well, *hollow*."

"Hollow?"

"That's not right, because they also seem flat, almost as if they don't have any thickness. But they don't just seem empty. Sometimes I get the impression that they're not things at all, but *holes* . . . holes in reality. Except that, when they move, the things that were behind them become visible again. Their presence doesn't seem to change anything. Sometimes, I think that they're just distortions, not so much holes in reality as wrinkles. This isn't really helping, is it? But if you see them in the same way . . . ?" She left the invitation dangling.

"Broadly, yes," he said, "but I was more inclined to use the analogy of lenses than wrinkles. Tell me, though—I couldn't see any sign of them in the paintings I saw yesterday, but have you tried to draw or paint them?"

She hesitated. "In a way," she said.

"What way?"

"I did try to replicate them, but I couldn't do it. I couldn't produce an image that replicated them accurately, but I did eventually produce . . . well something like them, but not quite the same."

"I don't understand," Adrian admitted.

"Nor do I, really. I can't explain it. I'd have to show you."

"In the barn."

"Yes—I suppose I'll have to, but I really don't want to. I'm scared, now, of what you might think . . . what you might think of me . . . if I show you. I will, for sure . . . but it's not easy. It's not finished. I don't think I'd have finished it anyway, to tell you the truth, but now—now that I know that someone will actually be able to see it, in its entirety—and that the someone in question is you, who will also be able to analyze and understand it . . . I'm not at all sure that I want it to be seen, that I want it to be analyzed and understood. I called you a coward yesterday, in a fit of temper, but I really didn't mean you. I meant me. I'm the coward. When I started the picture, I knew what I wanted to do. I still do . . . but I'm not sure, any more, that I should have wanted it, and after what you said yesterday, I'm certain that you'll think that I shouldn't. Perhaps I shouldn't care about that, and perhaps it's a weakness that I do, but I do."

Adrian didn't feel particularly flattered by that admission. He knew that it wasn't really a compliment to him. The simple fact of realizing that somebody else would see the aspects of her work that were secret, only supposed to be perceived subliminally, had forced her to think again about what she was doing, and whether she wanted to be seen to be doing it. That was only natural—and not really the focal point of his own interest. What interested him, for the moment, was the slight differences between her account of the elusive shadows and the one he'd compiled for himself, and the enigma of what those differences might signify.

"On your way down the hill," he asked, "Did you see any elusive shadows?"

"There was one at the back of the house," he said. "There always seems to be one in the vicinity of the barn. But I didn't see any as I was coming down the slope. It is dark, though—they're not easy to see, even for us. I often have the impression that the ones we glimpse are the exceptions, and that most of them are invisible . . . and that the ones I see only allow themselves to be glimpsed inadvertently, and deliberately disappear as soon as I reveal by looking at them that I'm aware of their presence."

"Which is inconvenient," Adrian pointed out, "because it will make it very difficult, when we try the experiment, to determine whether the entities we're seeing are the same ones. The descriptions tally well enough, but if they really are optical illusions, we wouldn't necessarily see them in the same apparent location, whereas, if they actually have some physical reality, we'd be both able to see them at the same time, in the same place."

"True," she admitted. "We do need to try that—but as you say, it might be difficult. Frustratingly difficult. Do you think their tendency to disappear proves that they *are* only optical illusions? I've often wished that I could actually convince myself of that, rather than suspecting that they're demonic lurkers always watching me, letting me catch teasing glimpses of them in order to taunt me?"

"I don't know," Adrian said. "As you say, it might be the more reassuring hypothesis, but I don't know. If they are real, they're certainly peculiar, only visible peripherally . . . or liminally. They only become visible at all because they modify the color of whatever is behind them, like inefficient chameleons—or what they're projected upon, if they really are shadows of some sort. In daylight, they can modify the blue of the sky or a lake, the greens of vegetation, and the grays of concrete, but they certainly seem to be more abundant when they're modifying the blacks of darkness. Is that because there are more of them about by night, or because our vision becomes more sensitive to them in conditions of limited light? I don't know—but it's certainly why they seem to be so closely akin to shadows, and why they might so readily suggest the idea of ghosts, or even demons . . ."

"Do you get the impression that they're *alive*, Adrian?" she asked, the urgency of the question causing her to interrupt. "Might they really be *watching* us?"

"I don't think so," he said, not simply by way of reassurance, "any more than shadows cast by the sun are alive and watching us, although they can sometimes give that impression."

"But if they are shadows of some sort, do you think that whatever might be casting them might be alive . . . and using them to watch us?"

"I'm wary of the analogy, but I can't rule it out conclusively . . . and while we're only talking about impressions, I do often get the impression that, although they're not living organisms in themselves, they're associated somehow with something alive. That might be purely subjective, though. You get the same feeling, obviously."

"And how. And more . . . worse."

"Worse?"

She hesitated. "This really might be paranoia, but I don't just get the feeling that there's something alive out there, something of which we can only see the shadows, but that it's something aware of us . . . that the reason the shadows are so elusive is that whatever there is out there really is hiding, *lying in wait*. Is it just paranoia? Fear born of superstition?"

Adrian hesitated, but felt that it was not an occasion for dissimulation. "I don't know," he said. "I'd be a liar if I said that I didn't have the same impression, but I really am inclined to attribute it to innate paranoia rather than genuine intuition. Sometimes I have to remind myself that whatever they are, they don't seem to be very substantial, and that they can't possibly pose any kind of physical threat. Have you ever seen one moving over your own body?"

"Only once. It felt creepy at the time, but I'm sure that was purely a psychological reaction, and that it didn't give rise to any actual touch sensations."

"But they do only seem to move over surfaces? You've never had the impression of anything moving through you . . . or, for that matter, anything else?"

She had to think about that, but eventually, she said: "That's right. They always do seem to be moving *over*, not *into*, as actual shadows do. Unless, when they disappear they do it by moving into whatever they're resting upon, dissolving into it. I suppose it's more akin to looking through a soft lens, although that's not exactly the kind of effect I've tried to duplicate in my painting."

"The painting in the barn?" Adrian queried.

Angelica pursed her lips slightly. "That's right," she said. "As I said, what I've done isn't a straightforward representation . . . more of an interpretation. What I've depicted might be quite different from the real thing.

172

But it had to be, because I couldn't make it disappear when I look at it . . . or when you look at it . . . if you look at it. I suppose you do want to, although you said no yesterday."

"I didn't think you were really offering to show it to me."

"I wasn't," she admitted. "If you'd said yes, I'd have made an excuse. I always have one ready—and it's true that it really isn't finished . . . and perhaps it never will be. I suppose I'll have to show it to you anyway . . . but have you thought of the possible danger of that—and of *this*?"

"Danger?" he repeated, interrogatively. It wasn't, strictly speaking, a lie.

"Don't be disingenuous, Adrian. You know what I mean, even if you don't feel it the way I do. If they *are* alive, *are* hiding, *lying in wait*, they might not want to be discovered and analyzed. It's probably irrelevant to them that we catch glimpses, as long as those glimpses are essentially frustrating, and we can't even be sure of them ourselves, let alone have any possibility of persuading anyone else that we can see them. But once I started trying to paint them, to depict them, that opened up the possibility of a discovery of sorts . . . the possibility that someone else might recognize what I'd depicted. And now there are two of us, comparing notes, making a concerted effort to analyze what we see, to comprehend it . . . So far as I can tell, there are none in the room right now, just as there didn't seem to be any when I was coming down the hill . . . but that doesn't mean that they can't see us and hear us. Or is that just paranoia?"

173

"Not *just* paranoia," Adrian admitted. "Yes it has occurred to me that we might be under observation—that the odd behavior of the elusive shadows might somehow be explicable in those terms. But if they really are optical instruments of some kind, allowing whatever produces them to catch glimpses of us, the fact remains that they're insubstantial in themselves. They can't actually touch us. They can't pose any physical danger to us."

"You can't be sure of that," Angelica countered, bluntly.

She was right, Adrian knew. He couldn't. If there were any truth at all in the hypothesis, then it opened up all kinds of potentially disturbing corollaries. If the elusive shadows were not only being cast but deliberately and purposively cast, who could tell what else their casters might be able to do, or want to do?

But it didn't seem to him to be the likeliest hypothesis, by any means.

"Even if the elusive shadows are being cast," he said, "it's highly unlikely that they're being cast by intelligent entities. If they really are shadows of a sort, the first question that needs to be asked, before exploring more fanciful hypotheses, is *where from?*"

"Another dimension?" she said, immediately. Modern occultists, including would-be witches, inevitably drew upon that vocabulary, albeit without any mathematical rigor.

"Possibly," he conceded, "but let's not go too far into the realms of speculation too quickly. As I said before, it's best to start with the basics, and now that we've done that, it's a good idea to consider what we've said very carefully. The main reason that I've been so eager to collect your impressions is that you're an artist, and doubtless have a much more fully-developed visual imagination than I have. As a scientist, I tend to think primarily in verbal and mathematical terms—when I design molecules in my head, it's more an exercise in geometry than picturing. Because the elusive shadows are essentially liminal, disappearing whenever I try to focus on them, I can't form any kind of visual image of them at all. I'm only aware of the shifts in coloration they induce. When it comes to shape and structure, I only get the vaguest impressions . . . but you've obviously *some* impression, however vague, of their form and make-up, in order to depict something like them. I need to see that."

"Not now," she said, immediately. "It's late. There isn't time."

"When?"

"Soon. I don't know yet. Jason's a problem in more ways than one. You might be disappointed, though. My painted images aren't an accurate representation—at least some of the features I depict are my projections—and having made them, I now see the real thing through the filter of those inventions, so even what I've told you tonight might not be the way they really are."

"I understand that," Adrian assured her. "But your observations still constitute valuable data—and so do your painted images."

She laughed, briefly but humorlessly. "You might think so . . . and you might be right . . . but you might get more than you bargained for, even though it isn't finished. Perhaps that's all the more reason why you ought to see it. I need to think like a scientist—like you—and just see it as an experiment. You'll probably be disappointed, though, and so will I. However it turns out, I suspect we'll both have been hoping for more."

"Everyone always hopes for more," Adrian said, "and it sometimes leads them to undervalue what they have—I'll try not to make that mistake. And let's not underestimate what we've achieved tonight. Simply bringing what we've seen into the open, confirming its similarities as well as its slight differences, has been an enormously helpful exercise. There really is a certain comfort to be drawn from the fact of not being alone, Mrs. Jarndyke, and the discussion we've just had really has made the elusive shadows an order of magnitude less elusive . . . and hopefully, less alarming. Don't you feel that?"

She looked him in the eyes, her gaze no longer piercing. "Not yet," she admitted. "I think I'm still too wound up. But you're probably right—when I get my equilibrium back, things will seem different . . . better. I just have to stop thinking of you as something disconcerting, and start thinking of you as an ally. You are an ally, Adrian, aren't you?"

"Absolutely. We are very definitely on the same side, facing the same predicament—together, if that's what we decide. I can't give you any answers yet, but I can copy you in on my quest to try to make sense of it all. It might seem tediously technical and more than a little pedantic, but there might be a measure of reassurance even in that."

She nodded her head. "There might," she admitted. She hesitated, and then said: "I can't provide any kind of *quid pro quo*, though. You do understand that?"

"Of course," Adrian said. "But might I point out that, like Meryl, you're missing the point. You've already provided a *quid pro quo*, simply by existing, simply by being prepared to collaborate. To be honest, I think I'm getting far more out of all of this than either you or Meryl ever will. I'm the one who's indebted, not you."

"You really believe that, don't you?" she said, after a pause.

"Of course."

"Well, for me, I'm glad—or will be. But don't try too hard to persuade yourself that you're exploiting Meryl while she thinks that she's exploiting you. She's not a whore, any more than I am, whatever people might think . . . and whatever she might think. I was watching you yesterday, not her, but I caught glimpses enough to get the impression that she's almost as besotted with you as you are with her. Trust me on that— I'm a woman as well as an artist, and I see all sorts of things to which men are utterly blind." She stood up. "I'd better get back to the barn now. Jason's always scrupulously careful of my privacy, while he thinks I'm working, but if I had to bet, I'd guess that he already has a duplicate key to the barn, and curiosity sometimes gives him itchy fingers.

Adrian stood up too. "We're not actually doing anything wrong, Mrs. Jarndyke," he reminded her.

"No, we're not," she agreed, as she picked up her cape and pulled the hood over her head. "But you can call me Angie anyway, if you like. Are you going to tell Meryl that you've seen me?"

"Yes, but I'll swear her to secrecy."

She was already on her way to the door of the apartment, but she turned round to nod her head. "Probably wise," she said. "Honesty is the best policy, they say . . . but then, *they*'re such liars that you can never trust them. If we're going to continue this conversation indefinitely, I suppose I'll have to tell Jason eventually . . . but not tonight. Is that all right?"

"He won't hear a whisper from me," Adrian promised.

After Adrian had checked that there was no one about, they slipped down the stairs quietly. No one saw them. The concierge was in his basement apartment, doubtless ready to respond to a summons if necessary, but hoping that none would come. On the broad doorstep of the building Angelica immediately stepped sideways, out of the cone of light projected by the porch light and into the shadows. She paused before gliding away into the darkness, though, in order to look out into the night, carefully, searching for something.

"Nothing?" she asked Adrian.

He too had taken a long look around. "Nothing," he confirmed. "But eventually, we'll be able to put it to the test. Let's be patient."

She had one more thing to say.

"I *do* feel better," she said. "I wasn't sure that I would, or even that I could, but I do. Good night, Adrian."

"Good night," he said, politely—but by the time he added "Angie," she had already vanished.

He went back upstairs and into the apartment. He stepped into his bedroom, but didn't switch the electric light on. He looked through the window, into the night, but there was no sign of Angelica Jarndyke in any of the pools of light projected by the street lights. The gloom beyond the pools of light was replete with darker shadows, one of which might have hidden her fugitive form. He searched them, too, for shadows that weren't "real" shadows at all: modifications of black on black: perverse lenses which did not magnify or bring anything closer, but managed nevertheless to signify that the world was a fuller and more complex entity than the sight of most naked eyes was able to apprehend. He couldn't discern anything—but he knew that that didn't necessarily mean that there was nothing there.

Adrian drew the curtains to protect himself from any eyes that might be lurking outside, unseen but attentive. Then he went back into the living room and sat down at his desk. Before he could apply his fingers to his keyboard, though, his phone beeped.

It was Meryl.

"The thing's over," she said. "I'm on my way home. Just ringing to say good night. Have you been lonely without me?"

"Of course."

"Good. Hold that regret. Pick you up tomorrow at seven?"

"Absolutely."

"Good. Good night, then."

"Good night," he echoed. He waited until the phone was closed before adding, in a whisper: "Love you." He had no idea at all how to attach a percentage to the probability that she might be doing the same, but he wasn't confident, in spite of what Angelica had said.

12

It was Friday afternoon before Jason Jarndyke dropped in on Adrian at the lab again, ostensibly for an update on the new batch of experiments that he had launched during the week.

"Promising, so far," Adrian reported. "A long way to go yet, though. I might have a design for the basic yellow, which is the first step toward the gold, but that remains to be tested. The basic red looks good in the dish. The violet seems to be the sticking point, for the moment, but psychology suggests that violet is the least important of the colors. No one has any theory to account for that yet. Given that bees seem to like it so much, one might expect humans to have more easily identifiable subliminal reactions to it—but science will be a dull business if we ever run out of enigmas, so we ought to be grateful even for the trivial ones."

Jarndyke inspected all the Petri dishes lined up in the Constant Temperature cells, which now numbered hundreds, muttering: "Good, good," although there was little visible within them as yet to justify that judgment. He made the usual comment about the project being a marathon, not a sprint, to cover up his undue impatience, and also added that his spies were still assuring him that Adrian was still way ahead of the competition, before saying: "Are you still seeing Meryl?"

"Yes," Adrian replied, without elaboration.

"Going well?" Jarndyke asked, evidently dissatisfied with the bald fact.

"Very well. I haven't been working nearly as hard out of hours for the last fortnight, although why you should be glad to hear me say that, I really don't know."

"*Mens sana in corpore sano*," the Industrialist quoted. "Happiness is the foundation of productivity. I'm truly glad that it's working out. Angie's much better, by the way. She was a little off-color last weekend, I'm afraid, although she insisted that she had to show you her pictures. I think she's coming round to the idea that it's good to have someone else with second sight around. I think she likes you, which helps. Maybe you and Meryl can come up to the Manse one night next week, for a drink and a chat. I don't think Angie's ready to let anyone into the barn yet, but I'm sure you can find lots of things to talk about, arts-wise. It'll be over my head, but you needn't worry about that. If Angie's happy, and you're happy, I'm happy. One of us will give you a ring over the weekend. Mention it to Meryl, and we'll see how our schedules fit."

"I will," Adrian promised.

It did not take long thereafter for Chester Hu to slip into Adrian's lab and say: "Tell me to mind my own business, if you want, but was the boss just inviting you up to Bleak House for a third successive Sunday lunch? I only ask because it would be a record."

"No, he didn't," Adrian told him, with scrupulous honesty, and couldn't help adding: "It's perhaps as well, because I have plans this weekend."

"With the bird he fixed you up with?"

"That's right."

"He must be over the moon about that. Let's just hope that he isn't disappointed, if and when."

"If and when what?" Adrian asked.

"Oh, well, you know what they say. The only good thing about love is that it doesn't usually last any longer than the common cold."

"Yes," said Adrian, mildly, "but *they're* such liars that one can't take anything they say seriously, can one?"

"Always been true in my case, alas," remarked Chester, wistfully. "But I wish you the best of luck, if that's what you want."

"Thank you very much."

There was hardy any gap before Chester was replaced by Martin Rutledge. "Don't take any notice of Chester," he advised. "A man who spends so much time playing *go* with the Koreans and always losing can't be reckoned a sound source of advice. How's the gold coming along."

"It's not, yet," Adrian admitted. "I might have a lead, though. With luck, I'll have a design to put into the DNA-synthesizer this time next week. After that, time will tell whether it's forward ho to the next ladder or back to square one."

"The red looks good, though," Rutledge commented, poring over the relevant Petri dishes in the relevant CT cell.

"Promising," Adrian admitted, "but a long way to go yet."

"And the boss doubtless told you that it's a marathon, not a sprint, while biting his fingernails down to the knuckle?"

"Something like that."

"Well, we're all rooting for you. We've all been caught up, or even overtaken, in our respective specialties, if the boss's spies can be trusted, but you seem to have a clear lead on the field, for now. We're all looking to you to pull the team over the finish line. No pressure, mind."

"None felt," Adrian assured him.

"And don't let Chester tell you that you ought to keep your mind on your work. The boss knows best. If he reckons it's best for his boys to be getting their end away regularly, he's sure to have done the research and made the calculation. Just do what you feel, and the hell with the naysayers."

"That was my plan," Adrian confirmed.

"Great. Have a good weekend."

A full quarter of an hour elapsed before the third wise man put in an appearance. He, too, complimented the red dots in the Petri dish, but did not bother to ask solicitously about the quest for gold. Instead, he said: "I've been reading up about purple. Did you know that imperial purple wasn't really purple at all?"

"Yes," said Adrian. "The phrase was metaphorical. The dye that the Romans used to color imperial trappings was actually more like crimson."

"This is more like poppy red," Horst Koerner observed, pointing at the Petri dishes.

"It is now," Adrian confirmed, "but it's a good root molecule. A couple of C to A and H to G substitutions, and a few extra hydroxyl groups on the pigment protein, and I should be able to segue into scarlet, and then into crimson, and half a dozen shades in between."

"Are there half a dozen shades in between?"

"Definitely. If you don't believe me, consult a bee."

"That won't be necessary. You must introduce me to your girl-friend, by the way."

"Why? So that you can give her a quick run-down of your ingenious psychological analysis of my character and try to poach her?"

"Of course not—you're my friend. So that I can give you a psychological analysis of her character and give you fair warning of her flaws."

"No need—she doesn't have any."

"A man in your condition always thinks his girl-friend has no flaws. That's why he needs the advice of a clinical eye."

"In my condition? What's my condition?"

"In love, of course. Do you think it isn't obvious? You're the talk of the biotech division: a geneticist in love. You can find unicorns in any petting zoo nowadays, but geneticists in love are still a genuine rarity. Of course, the general opinion is that you're just faking it to curry favor with the boss, because he fixed you up, but I know better. The others wouldn't know the real thing if it bit them in the balls, but I'm Viennese."

"And you wish me the best of luck, because we're all on the same team and you're all looking to me to pull the entire division, not to mention the Jarndyke Industries bank balance, way into the lead in the Great Race of Progress?"

"You know me so well—and on such a short acquaintance, too. You could almost be Viennese yourself."

"I'll take that as a compliment," Adrian said, dryly.

"There's none higher. But you really ought to introduce me to your girl-friend. A man in love can never have too much information, and you're not going to get a reliable opinion from anyone else in the building, believe me. They might be geniuses at genetics and go, but there's not one, except for you and me, who can tell Mozart from mozzarella."

"And not one, including you and me, who can tell modesty from millinery," Adrian observed, "but we all have our faults—except, of course, for my girl-friend."

Horst went away, shaking his head and smiling. Adrian still liked him, in spite of everything . . . or perhaps because of it.

When he arrived back at the apartment, Meryl was already there. He had given her a key the night before, and she had obviously been impatient to take advantage of the privilege. As soon as he appeared she drew him into the kitchen, so that she could start preparations for dinner with the various ingredients she'd bought. Adrian observed, as she popped it into the oven, that the half-shoulder of lamb came from a real sheep, not a tissue culture. He approved of that.

"I just got a phone call from Angelica Jarndyke," she said. "She says that Jayjay has ordered her to invite us over for drinks and a serious chat about art one evening next week. She's lying, obviously—it's her idea."

"Actually, Jayjay mentioned it to me this afternoon in the lab. He made it sound like his idea."

"Well, he had to, didn't he: Angelica's orders. I accepted for Wednesday. That's okay with you, isn't it?"

Adrian laughed. "At your orders," he said. "Between the two of you, I don't really have much of a say, do I?"

"Don't be like that," she replied, as she drew him into the dining room for an aperitif, as the vegetables that she had just finished rapidly peeling and trimming would not have to be put on to boil for an hour or so. "It's not for my benefit, is it? Don't you think it might be a little awkward, if Angelica hasn't told him that she came to see you on Monday. If we're going to be seeing them regularly, keeping secrets could lead to difficulties, especially if she's going to make a regular thing of dropping round for a chat. *Is* she going to make a regular thing of it?"

"I don't know," Adrian admitted. "But you're right, obviously. If she does, it could well lead to difficulties. What do you think I ought to do about it?"

Meryl put on a show of thinking about that, before saying: "I suppose there's not a lot you can do. It's probably better if I have a word with her. Hints are always better received coming from another woman. Not that she's likely to take any notice of me, mind."

"Maybe best to keep quiet and leave it up to her, then?" Adrian suggested.

"You would think that, I suppose. Personally, I don't understand why she hasn't told Jayjay. It's not as if the two of you have anything to hide, is it?"

Adrian was well aware that she was watching him like a hawk as she asked that question, and he was also well aware that his chances of cutting off the inquisition at that point were very slim.

"Actually," he said, "that's the problem. We do."

"What?" she said icily.

"Oh, not that," he said. "Definitely not that. But there's something that Angelica hadn't told Jayjay for years, and would probably never have told anyone if I hadn't appeared on the scene. As I told you, with perfect honesty, she came round to compare notes on what our extended sight had told us about the nature of the world. That's all we did. But Angelica couldn't tell Jayjay that without exciting further curiosity. It's not so much *what* she's been hiding from him as the simple fact that she's been hiding it—not just for two weeks, the way I've been refraining from telling you about it, but for fifteen years. So yes, there already are difficulties, and I don't know how best she can sort them out . . . but we need to leave it up to her, and play along with whatever she decides."

There was a long pause then, while Meryl digested all the implications of that revelation.

"Well," she said, finally, "you and I have only known one another for a fortnight, and I certainly haven't opened my closet wide enough to show you all the skeletons inside, so I guess I'm not entitled to feel hurt the way that Jayjay would if he found that his wife of

fifteen years had been hiding something from him . . .
something important, I presume?"

"Important to her."

"Something to do with her depressions, and the reason that your arrival on the scene spooked her instead of making her throw her arms open in welcome?"

"Yes, indirectly."

"Something she could never tell anyone else, but felt compelled to tell you?"

"Something she felt that she had to check with me, just as I felt compelled to check with her. We both needed to know . . . to be sure."

"And have you ever told anyone about it, or am I a special case?"

"No, I haven't ever told anyone about it—for exactly the same reason that Angelica hasn't."

"And the two of you are going to take the secret to the grave, are you?"

"No, I don't think so. Now that there are two of us in it, the risk of being thought insane has diminished considerably—at least the danger of self-suspicion. Except that . . ."

"Except what?"

"If Angelica is still intent on keeping it secret, it puts a certain pressure on me to keep it too."

"Even from me?"

"Perhaps especially from you, if, as you say, the two of us are going to be seeing Jayjay regularly."

"Then why did you tell me the secret exists, you bloody fool? What effect do you think that's going to have on my curiosity—not to mention my trust?"

"Much the same effect as if I hadn't told you, and left you wondering why Angelica was so intent on keeping a meeting that was, in fact, perfectly innocent, secret from her husband."

Meryl weighed that up, and then said: "Do you think she knows what kind of awkward situation she's putting us in?"

"She's a very intelligent woman. Troubled, yes, but certainly capable of thinking things through while the balance of her mind isn't disturbed. If you're right about the invitation for next week being her idea and not Jayjay's it's possible that she intends to come clean, and wants us there for moral support, and for the benefit of my testimony that her behavior was understandable and excusable . . . but I don't know. She's a complicated woman as well as an intelligent one. It's not her fault—she's had a rougher time than I have, and I've been close enough to paranoia myself to know how much worse things could have become. As you've probably noticed, I'm no paragon of normalcy myself."

"You really do know how to wind a girl up, don't you?" she said, more than a trifle bitterly. "Beneath that innocent exterior . . . Am I a perfect fool, then, for . . . oh well, it wouldn't be the first time. You think you're in control of a situation, and then . . . the sinkhole opens up underneath you. But I haven't a leg to stand on, in more ways than one. So I have to wait until Wednesday, do I, with the frail hope that Angelica bloody Jarndyke might finally decide to confess all to her doting husband, to find out what's really going on?"

190

"Not necessarily," said Adrian, calmly—far more calmly than he actually felt, after hearing the ominous ellipses in Meryl's speech.

"What's that supposed to mean?"

"It mans that I'm toying with the idea of telling you, in spite of feeling a certain obligation to Angelica."

"Oh? Toying, you say?"

"Perhaps not the most apt description. Thinking. Trying to weigh up exactly how far I ought to trust you."

"That's a bastard thing to say. Do you think I'd blab, even if I crossed my heart and swore to keep your precious secret?"

"That's not what worries me."

"What is?"

"What you said a few minutes ago about not having opened your closet wide to let me see the skeletons inside. And something Horst Koerner said to me this afternoon about nobody in Jarndyke's entire biotech division knowing the real thing if it bit them in the balls. He kindly made me an exception as well as himself, but I have my doubts about him, and I certainly don't trust my own judgment."

After yet another pause, she said: "Okay, I'll trade. Do you want my entire life story in filthy detail, or is there something specific you have in mind?"

"Something specific."

"Which is?"

"I want to know the real reason why you took me home with you the Tuesday after we first met."

"Do you?" Again, she paused for thought, and then said: "Well I suppose if I were you, I would too, given that I came across as such a slut. But if I tell you, you have to promise to bear in mind that that was then and this is now. What was true then . . . well, things have moved on in a way I couldn't predict at the start. It might be best to let it lie . . . but I suppose I owe you the truth, if you want it. Honesty is the best policy, they say."

Adrian refrained from making any remark about the reliability of "they" and their sayings.

"That was then and this is now," he said. "Got it. Go on."

"It's not what you think—at least, it's not what you think if what you think is that I was just giving you a casual *quid pro quo* because you'd just agreed to give me a useful leg up with my dismal publications record. It was the way you did it."

"I don't understand," Adrian confessed.

"No, I know. Just like you didn't understand the night before, when I gave you an unnecessary lift home and you just got out of the car without showing the slightest flicker of interest. I'd already decided by then, of course, to try to pump you about your theories and perceptions, for anything I might be able to apply to my own field, but I'd assumed that it would be easy, even though I'm a couple of years older than you and can't hold a candle to Angelica bloody Jarndyke, looks-wise. If anything, I thought that if she'd got you hot, you'd be even more likely to try to hit on me. But nothing. I had to bully you into asking me out—and then, same again. Not a flicker. When I fluttered my eyelashes and proposed that we collaborate, you just said yes, as if it were a matter of no importance whatsoever, like throwing a bone to a dog.

"I wouldn't say that I'm particularly insecure person but . . . well, I am pushing thirty, nearly, and I've fallen into a sinkhole or two in my time. So I said to myself: I'll make the snotty little sod fall in love with me even if I have to fuck his brains out to do it. Or unvoiced words to that effect. But it all went horribly wrong. Even while we were actually doing it, it was as if you were hardly even there. Not the reaction I was looking for—and my own reaction certainly wasn't. I thought if I hooked you, landing you wouldn't be difficult. Wrong. And I thought that whatever happened, I'd be safe on the bank with dry feet. Wrong again. Only went and hooked myself. Honestly, sometimes, I think I'm just a walking bloody cliché. Instead of making you fall in love with me, I hoist myself with my own bloody petard.

"So here I am, hovering over the sinkhole again, pathetically dependent on yet another man who really doesn't care about me one way or another, even if he continues to tolerate me, even to the extent of chucking me a key to his apartment like tossing another bone to the dog. So now you know what happened. But that was then and this is now, and, as they used to say way back when, a fortnight is a long time in politics."

"*They* say a lot of stupid things," Adrian muttered, reflexively, before gathering his courage together and hastening to say: "It was all my fault. I *was* interested—

extremely interested—but I didn't dare let it show. It hasn't been nearly as bad for me as it has for Angelica, but I've still had twenty years to form a habit of keeping all my cards exceedingly close to my chest and laying them out one by one with the utmost prudence. As you observed at the time, I hadn't ever been on a date before. I hadn't ever been given an unnecessary lift home by an attractive woman before. I didn't have any script to go on, so I followed my own customary protocol, and pretended that I was made of stone. As for the next night, the reason I seemed detached was because I'd never actually done it before, and I was monitoring myself with extreme care, hoping that I wouldn't do anything stupid or get taken by surprise.

"It wasn't you who weren't making an impression, and I wasn't so much cool as petrified. You could probably have made me fall head over heels in love with you just by fluttering your eyelashes a few more times, or without even bothering to do that—although the other method worked just as well. And as you say, this is now, and here we are, both suspended over the sinkhole by our crossed wires, and trying hard not to let on because we're afraid . . . and both failing to see what is apparently perfectly obvious to everybody else, even biotech geeks who can't tell Mozart from mozzarella."

"Oh," said Meryl.

"They also say, so I'm told, that the best thing about love is that it doesn't usually last longer than the common cold—which just goes to prove that biotech geeks aren't the only ones who don't know Mozart from mozzarella. I can't guarantee that now is forever, but I'm perfectly certain that it's going to last a lot longer than next Wednesday night, at least on my part."

She thought about that for a moment or two, and then said: "And mine. But I'd better go put the vegetables on, or the lamb will be overdone. Open that bottle of wine I brought, will you? I think we could both use another drink."

Adrian opened the bottle of Wiltshire red, and then carved the meat, making a terrible mess of hacking it away from the bone, but producing a sufficient number of edible shards. Then, as they ate, he told Meryl the full story of the elusive shadows, and why they, far more than the ability to perceive additional colors, had caused him to fear being thought insane . . . and, indeed, to fear that he might, perhaps, be seeing things that were entirely a product of a mind gone astray.

"I coped with that uncertainty," he concluded. "So did Angelica, in her own way—but it was harder for her. You can see, can't you, why she never told her husband? And why, when the possibility of the truth finally being laid bare suddenly became urgent, she was . . . and still is . . . less than delighted?"

"But that was then," Meryl observed. "This is now . . . and things are different now."

"Perhaps they are," Adrian agreed. "Time will tell."

13

"Okay," said Meryl, when they were on the last glass of wine, and had moved from the ravaged dining table to the armchairs. "What are they, your elusive shadows?"

"I don't know. If I did, they wouldn't be elusive, and I wouldn't have been frightened for the last ten years and more that if I let on to anyone that I could see them I'd collect a diagnosis of schizophrenia and never be employable as long as I lived. Far better to be a taciturn genius who keeps his delusions bottled up than a crazy one who lets them all hang out."

"But you must have a theory?"

"Not really. On the other hand, by applying the scientific method, I did make a great deal more intellectual progress than poor Angelica, when she was young and impressionable. At least I eliminated several hypotheses from consideration that continued haunting her mind for a long time . . . and still do, I suspect."

"Ghosts? Evil spirits? Monsters from the nth dimension?"

"Ghosts and evil spirits, yes . . . although, as I mentioned to Angelica, it's not impossible that glimpses of the elusive shadows by seers in the past made some contribution to the growth and proliferation of the legendry of ghosts and demons. Monsters from the nth dimension . . . that I'm not so sure that I can eliminate."

"Really?"

"I fear so. You see, the shadows do resemble shadows in some significant ways, particularly the fact that they appear to have no third dimension, and the fact that they're only visible because they interfere with the information that light would normally transit to the eyes from the objects behind them. But if they are shadows of some sort, that raises the question of what could be casting them. If they were solid objects in normal space, they'd presumably be at least as visible as the shadows, but they're not.

"That opens the possibility that they might be more like images projected by a lens. If they were always bright, that would be an attractive idea, especially as we know that air can sometimes function as if it were a lens, in projecting mirages and rainbows, without the lens being visible. In fact, though, the elusive shadows are often dark, and seem to be more abundant at night, as shades of black on black. That doesn't necessarily eliminate the possibility of some kind of refractive phenomenon, but the problem remains of where the object whose image is being refracted might be, and where the refractive lens might be. In any case, that wasn't the first set of explanatory hypotheses that I tried to explore, and that wasn't the framework of my thinking when I was in the experimental phase of my enquiry."

"The experimental phase?"

"Of course. I'm a scientist—although, admittedly, when that phase began, I was a teenager, and that might have had more to do with the active approach I took to the problem."

"You mean that you tried to catch one of the shadows? To capture one for study?"

"Exactly. In fact, to begin with—I was a teenager, remember—my first approach was rather more brutal than that. The first thing I tried to do was to pin one down. I didn't have a bow and arrow, and wouldn't have been able to shoot straight if I had, but I did have a set of darts, and I could at least hit a dartboard, even getting reasonably close to the bull's eye. But that was when I first began to think of the entities as *elusive* shadows. Catching sight of them is difficult enough, and they seem to vanish as soon as you try to look at them directly, let alone throw a dart at them. So, I quickly decided that the first thing to do was trying to lure them closer—as close as possible, maybe even close enough to grab one with my hands.

"I won't bore you with the various phases of what turned out to be an utterly futile series of exercises. I soon got bored with lying very still and hoping that they might simply wander across me, and my attempts to figure out whether they preferred some surfaces to others, in the hope that I might be able to find something that could qualify as bait for a trap never got much beyond the broad observation that they seemed to like night better than day and outside far better than inside."

"You were assuming at the time that they were alive, and even intelligent?" Meryl queried.

"At the time, yes. The very fact that they seemed to flee direct gaze seemed to imply a purpose in their behavior. Brutal as my approach was in those days, my vague dream wasn't to kill one of them, but to be able to make contact with them, not necessarily to establish communication—their behavior seemed more reminiscent of house-flies than sciencefictional aliens—but just to be able to touch them. And then I read *Flatland*, and my attitude underwent a drastic paradigm-shift."

"What's *Flatland*?"

"It's a fantasy by a Victorian mathematician about a two-dimensional world populated by squares, triangles and other geometrical shapes, describing their perceptions and their movements, and a social hierarchy based on the number of angles they have. Until then, I'd been thinking of the shadows simply as being very thin. I hadn't given much thought to the implications of the possibility that they were literally two-dimensional, actually devoid of thickness. In the original *Flatland*, the two-dimensional world in which the squares and triangles live really is flat: a seemingly infinite plane. But other mathematicians took the fantasy further; one wrote a story in which the two-dimensional universe is the surface of a sphere, and thus finite, like the Earth. And it immediately occurred to me that the surface of the sphere didn't have to be smooth, like a billiard-ball—that it could be as complex topologically as the actual surface of the Earth. That seemed to connect so well with what little I'd been able to observe of the behavior of the elusive shadows that I immediately jumped to the conclusion that what I was seeing was actually a two-dimensional universe distributed over the surface of the Earth, and inhabitants analogous to the squares and triangles of the Victorian Flatland."

"Inhabitants that avoid contact with the weird three-dimensional monsters over and under their thin universe," said Meryl, having no difficulty following the argument as soon as it was explained, "because it would be inconvenient for them if, say, one of the horrible things stuck a dart through them? That's why they prefer the dark to the light and avoid the insides of the labyrinthine caves where the three-D monsters live?"

"That was my initial thinking, practically word for word," Adrian agreed. "Although it didn't take me long to realize that it couldn't be nearly as simple as that."

"Because the elusive shadows weren't just avoiding contact with you, but actually dodging your gaze?"

"That as well, but what captured my attention more was the slit problem."

"Which is?"

"Imagine a shadow cast on the ground by some moving solid object—a flying bird, say. As it travels, it comes to the door of a house. What does it do?"

"It travels up the door."

"Exactly. But if an elusive shadow isn't something cast by a distant object, but something entirely independent, with a life of its own, what happens when it comes to the same door—assuming that there's a crack, however thin, at the bottom of the door?"

"It goes under the door, like a trickle of liquid. So that test would be able to tell you whether your elusive shadows really are shadows of some sort, or . . . fluid flatlanders in a bumpy flatland?"

"If only it had been that simple. Again, I won't bore you with the problem of actually trying to catch one of the bastards, from the corner of my eye, approaching a door, but I did, in fact, manage to do it eventually. Long before then, though, I'd realized that it wasn't going to help, because I'd already seen, hundreds of times, without actually thinking about it, elusive shadows moving over surfaces that contained all kinds of cracks and fissures of various dimensions. I already knew that, rather than one or the other, the elusive shadows could do either: that they could behave as if they were shadows, or as if they were liquid."

"They make a choice, you mean?"

"Not necessarily. They might be entirely passive entities, simply responding to circumstance. But what it does mean is that if they really are in a two-dimensional far-from-flatland, that two-dimensional universe is not merely bumpy, as you put it, but . . . well, initially I thought *flexible*, or *versatile*, but it's not even as simple as that. I suspect that the best analogy might be *uncertain*, as in the context of Heisenberg's uncertainty principle."

"You mean that when an elusive shadow approaches a door, it can go either up or under, depending on how the two-D universe . . . solidifies at that particular moment in time?"

"If it is always a matter of either/or, yes. Sometimes, perhaps, it might even do both."

Meryl laughed. "Is that how your elusive shadows reproduce, then?"

"I don't know. I've been catching glimpses for a long time now, but I've never glimpsed one undergoing binary fission, and I've certainly never seem two of them engaging in anything that might qualify as sexual intercourse."

"Well, they are shy, according to your account. They don't like being looked at—but surely that's a more important point than you seem to think. If they're in a two-D universe, however bumpy, how can they be aware of anything that's going on in the third dimension? And even if they're aware of the movement of solid objects in that third dimension, one way or another, how can they possibly be aware of merely being an object of a gaze . . . your very special gaze, of which only one in maybe ten million people appear to be capable?"

"Indeed. And that's exactly why, until a few days ago, I thought that by far the greater probability was that the whole two-dimensional universe had to be a fantasy, and that the elusive shadows were highly likely to be a subjective phenomenon, seemingly fleeing my gaze by vanishing for exactly the same reason as spots that appear to be before the eyes that are really on the surface or actually inside the eyeball."

"But now you've met Angelica, and she can see them too."

"Now I've met Angelica, and although it might take days of discussion, or weeks, to figure out exactly how closely our experiences tally, I've already managed to ascertain that they're similar enough to imply that there really is something out there, however paradoxical it might seem."

"Something that, if its components really are avoiding your touch, your gaze and your investigation, is aware of your existence . . . and your interest."

"Probably—or maybe just perhaps. I haven't really had a chance to think that one all the way through yet. Too many distractions. Work—and other things."

"You really do need to practice your flattery. I don't want to be just *another thing*."

"Sorry."

"Apology accepted." Another thought evidently occurred to Meryl then. "But while that's a conclusion you're only coming to reluctantly, having kept it at bay for years, it's one that Angelica jumped to a long time ago, and has been living with for all, or most of her life. No wonder the poor woman's paranoid."

"Indeed."

"But they've never actually done anything to either of you? They've never even tried to touch you?"

Adrian grimaced. "I don't know. I asked her, naturally, but she answered warily, although she did say that she once saw one flow over her body, which I never have, as yet . . . although it doesn't mean that none ever has. Although it was probably just natural paranoia, I sometimes had a suspicion when I was younger that they might be flowing over me while I was asleep, or lurking on my back where I couldn't see them. I managed to set it aside. Perhaps she hasn't."

"But even if they do flow over you, could they actually do anything to you? Could they even make tactile contact, however slightly?"

"I don't know. And the possibilities don't stop there."

Again, Meryl was quick on the uptake. "The slit problem!" she said. "They wouldn't necessarily be limited to flowing *over* you. They could also flow *inside*?"

"Perhaps."

"Shit! Did you tell Angelica that?"

"No. But it does put me in something of a quandary, as you can imagine. On Monday, she was the only person in the world to whom I could talk about this—and already, I'm setting things aside because I don't want to frighten her, keeping secrets from her."

"But you're telling me. I'm flattered . . . or am I? You're telling me now, obviously, although you've never told anybody before, because it's only now that you feel that you have the endorsement necessary for you to take the story seriously yourself, and you're telling me because I'm the only person close enough to the events of the last couple of weeks to be able to take that endorsement entirely seriously, and not suspect that you're simply off your rocker. It's not because you have any particular respect for my intelligence, or because we're . . . involved. I just happened to be in the relevant place at the relevant time."

Adrian sighed. "I've just told you that there's a theoretical possibility that two-dimensional succubi creep inside our bodily orifices by night while we're asleep, perhaps in legions, and the only kind of insecurity you can muster is to question my motives for telling you, in case they don't fit your notion of a perfect romance?"

Meryl looked daggers at him. "Fair point," she conceded, eventually. "Cruel, but fair. And you're right, of course—any sanely paranoid person would be wondering, with a shudder, how many elusive shadows might have crept inside me last night, and are now neatly ensconced in my brain, parasitizing my eyesight and my feelings. *How* long have you been thinking about this sort of thing?"

"This particular idea, not that long. And it's only a hypothesis, resident in the far reaches of unlikelihood. Lots of people entertain far nastier hypotheses far more seriously on a daily basis without going mad. You have to remember that I'm always forced to the eventual conclusion that I don't really know anything for sure, and that my decade-long quest to discover more, even with the aid of the scientific method and an intellect reputed to be genius level, has been very slow and deeply frustrating. Jason Jarndyke would doubtless clap me on the shoulder and tell me not to worry, because it's a marathon not a sprint, but every time he says that to me, I can't help remembering that the runner featured in Plutarch's original anecdote dropped dead as soon as he arrived in Athens.

"In recent years, in fact—at least since I started my PhD and found myself in intimate confrontation with the infinite possibilities of genetic engineering, and the practical spinoff of engineering pigmentation genes and integrating them into artificial genomes—I'd almost given up thinking about it, except in idle moments. I stopped trying to pin the elusive shadows down, and even stopped trying to observe them in any kind of disciplined way. Tacitly, I'd accepted that the enigma was insoluble, and that as my life could proceed perfectly well while ignoring it, that was the sane thing to do. Then I met Angelica, and saw her painting of Hell."

"And me," Meryl reminded him. "Although, now you've filled in the back-story, I'm beginning to understand why you didn't react as any normal man would when I tried to provoke you with my inept feminine wiles."

"You were—are—a godsend," Adrian said. "Angelica . . . I'm not so sure. For better or worse, though, the problem is alive and kicking again, and it isn't going to go away. Nor is it simply a matter of exercising my imagination and my intellect. I actually have a real social situation to negotiate—never my forte—which involves my employer, who thinks I'm the key to delivering the Golden Fleece and making him billions, his wife, who is too beautiful and too neurotic by at least half, and my first ever girl-friend, acquired by means of a whirlwind romance. Compared with all that, the problem of fleeting glances of a parallel two-dimensional universe would seem trivial, if they weren't at the very heart of the real-world problem."

"Three hours ago, I thought you were a godsend too," Meryl murmured. "At least, I hoped you were. Now . . . well, I still do, I suppose. I might need time to think before I can decide whether I ought to be grateful to Eros for hurling me into your skinny arms or cursing him for one more ironic joke. No . . . forget I said that. It's bad enough being a cow without being a cow queuing up at the abattoir. I'm hooked on you, you're hooked on me, at least for the time being—at the end of the day, what else really matters? What I really need to do is not to think about it, and fortunately, I know a way of doing that. I'm not fit to drive though—we're going to have to make do with that ridiculously narrow bed of yours. You really ought to get a double. Show some commitment."

"I will," Adrian promised. He thought, however, that trying not to think about it all, even with the aid of the kind of distraction that Meryl could provide, wasn't going to be easy. "It's not that late, though, and it's Friday."

"So?"

"Friday's the day I skype my mother."

"Are you saying that you want me to leave the room?"

"No—the opposite. I want to introduce you to her, and tell her that we're together. Show some commitment."

"Oh. Do you think she'll approve?"

"She'll be over the moon. Give her five minutes to get over the shock, and she'll be dreaming about grandchildren."

"Does this mean that I have to introduce you to my parents? They ought to be over the moon, given that I'm dating the man who's going to deliver the Golden Fleece to Jason Jarndyke, but they're a bit unpredictable."

"No rush," Adrian told her. "When you're ready. We have all the time in the world."

14

When Wednesday evening arrived, as it did, inexorably, Adrian felt that he was still somewhat at sea, not having made a definite decision, or even identified a clear inclination, but he felt a certain calmness nevertheless, simply because he had no control over the situation. It was out of his hands; decisions, for the moment, were Angelica Jarndyke's province. She had not come to the apartment again, but he did not suppose for a moment that that was because she had no more questions to ask, and no longer felt any need for reassurance as to her sanity. Indeed, given that she was an intelligent woman, he assumed that as soon as she had accepted the present situation and absorbed the scant information he had given her regarding his own observation of the elusive shadows, she had begun to work out an entirely new set of anxious possibilities.

He assumed that, presumably having never encountered *Flatland* and its imaginative spinoff, she was probably not thinking in terms of two-dimensional universes parallel to the Earth's surface, but that still left a large number of potential conceptual frameworks. Perhaps she would revise and rejargonize the notion that the elusive shadows might be the souls of the dead, or that they were alien beings of some kind, made of ordinarily-dark matter, placidly sharing our space. Whichever way her imagination was leading her, however, the one thing about which Adrian felt certain was that her mind would not be inactive. Quite the contrary.

He nursed a vague hope that she might have taken advantage of Monday or Tuesday evening to bring her husband up to date with the secret she had been keeping for years and tell him about her nocturnal visit to his apartment, but he knew that it was a rather frail hope. She would wait for the moral support. She would want him there to back up her story—if, in fact, she had any intention of telling it.

He expected that there would be long preliminaries, as there had been on both the Sundays, but either Angelica was conscious of the limited time available after seven o'clock in the evening, or her impatience could no longer brook any further delay. Jason Jarndyke had scarcely poured the first round of drinks—brandies all round, Meryl having walked up the hill and Adrian having ordered a bed on-line on Saturday that had been delivered, assembled and installed in his bedroom on Monday while he was at work, under the attentive eye of the apartment-block's concierge—before Angelica claimed the floor and said:

"I'm afraid that I persuaded Jason to invite you both here tonight under slightly false pretences, and that I'm going to be rather rude. I'm sorry about this,

Meryl, but I wonder if you wouldn't mind keeping Jayjay company for half an hour or so, while I take Adrian away. I need to show him something, and to ask his advice about it."

The announcement obviously came as a surprise to Jason Jarndyke, who was the first to react: "You're going to show him the barn? Well, why don't we all come? I've been dying to see it for months . . . more than a year, now."

"That's exactly the point," said Angelica, quietly but firmly. "You *can't* see it. Quite literally. So far as I know, Adrian is the only person in the world who can. That's why I need to show it to him . . . and just to him, for the time being. I know that you can't quite understand, Jason, but I promise you that when I've discussed the matter with Adrian, one of us will try to explain. I know I ought to do it, but I'm not sure that I can, even if I can pluck up the courage. At any rate, one of us will fill you in, if you can be patient for a little while longer."

She shot Adrian a glance that might have been imploring, but it was a sideways glance, and her body-language was replete with embarrassment. She didn't wait for any kind of assent from him. It was Meryl she addressed next. "Will you forgive me, my dear?" she was asked.

"Of course," said Meryl.

What else could she say? Adrian thought

Angelica did not take Adrian's hand, or make any other gesture of guidance; she simply turned and went toward the door of the room, without even looking back to check that he was following her.

Adrian mumbled an apology of sorts to his astonished employer, shot an apologetic glance at Meryl,
and hastened to catch up with his hostess, carrying
his brandy glass carefully, although there was really
no possibility of any of the liquid splashing over the
high rim.

Angelica held the back door of the Manse open for
him, and then closed it behind them.

"Fuck," she murmured. "That was hard." Then she
looked up at Adrian. "You understand why this is hard,
don't you?"

"Yes," he said, simply. "It's okay. If you want me to
explain it to Jayjay, I will. Anything I can do to help."

She still hadn't moved in the direction of the barn,
which was about six hundred meters away, on the far
side of the garden, which was far from being in full
bloom, spring being insufficiently far advanced. She
was conscientiously not looking in that direction.
Although the equinox was imminent, the last of the
twilight had faded away some time ago, and it was
dark outside, but it was a clear night, and the moon
was three-quarters full. As Adrian's eyes adapted to the
gloom, he was able to see the contours of the buildings
and the plants clearly enough . . . as well as the elusive
shadow on the wall of the barn.

There was no reason for him to be surprised by its
presence, of course; Angelica had told him that she
glimpsed them frequently.

"Keep looking at me," she told him. "You can see
it, can't you?"

"Yes"

"Where, exactly?"

"Approximately two feet above the level of the lintel and maybe two meters to the right."

She exhaled. "Check," she said. "Now, one of us needs to look directly at it while the other holds it in the corner of the field of vision. Shall I look?"

"Fine."

"Okay. One, two, three . . . it's gone!"

"Indeed," Adrian confirmed.

"So it's not an optical illusion?"

"The experiment would suggest not," Adrian agreed.

"I'm not sure whether to be pleased about that or scared. You?"

"Ditto. Shall we move?"

She started to walk along a path that led through a small vegetable garden before becoming a brief avenue lined by box-trees with low, carefully-sculpted crowns, but she walked very slowly, evidently having something to say before they got there.

"They don't usually come into the barn," she said, "but they can, can't they? There's nothing to stop them. So they could see what's in there, if they wanted to."

"I'm not sure they can *see* anything at all, in a literal sense," Adrian told her. "They do seem to be able to sense human presence, even human attention, so perhaps they can, but I can't work out how."

"Might they be telepathic?"

"I find that even more implausible. Their reaction to direct gaze is certainly odd, and perhaps slightly worrying, but I don't think we should give in to the temptation to read too much into it. I really don't think that there's any need to be frightened of them, Mrs. Jarndyke."

"Angie," she corrected him. "You need to call me Angie. Please."

"Of course, Angie."

"I know I'm foolish. I know they've never hurt me, and will probably continue to make sure that they hardly ever so much as touch me. But if they did . . . it's like spiders. There's no real reason to be afraid of them, but I just can't help it. And if they know, somehow, that we know about them now, when we could never be sure before . . . well, I meant what I said inside. I need you to see the barn. I need to know what you think. Then . . . well, I'll try to tell Jayjay about the shadows myself, but I need you to be there, just in case I can't. If I have to ask you, you will, won't you?"

"Of course."

"Good . . .

"I'm a wreck," murmured Angelica, pausing on the path in order to make a longer speech. "And a liar too. Jayjay's going to be disappointed in me—just when I'm beginning to lose my qualifications as a trophy wife. But he's not going to throw me out. I know that. He's not a man to invest twenty years of patience and then blow it all in one fit of pique. You're lucky, you know, to have other things to pursue—Jason's blessed Golden Fleece. All I've had is the barn, and now . . . well you'll see in a minute. But you're lucky, too, that you're a scientist, and no one actually expects you to be happy. When you're a good-looking woman, people expect you to live up to the image—not just to want to be happy, but actually to *be* happy. I always feel that I'm somehow letting them down."

"I suppose that's true," Adrian agreed. "Scientists are expected to be eccentric, cynical and miserable. Nobody expects them to be happy. It's not an advantage for which I've ever felt particularly grateful, though."

"I suppose not. I get so wrapped up on my own problems that I tend to forget that other people just have different ones. But you're happy now, aren't you—with Meryl?"

"Yes."

"I missed out on that, a little," she mused, as she resumed walking. "When Jason and I first got together, we both had reasons that had nothing to do with love. I did learn to love him, over time, but . . . well, there have always been difficulties, only some of which you can guess. I shouldn't be envious, though. I know, intellectually, that you and Meryl probably have problems of your own, or will have. But for the moment, you're happy. That's something precious. Make the most of it."

They had reached the door of the barn, and Angelica inserted a key into one of two locks. She fumbled slightly over the second one, but it was by no means the first time she had undertaken the double operation in the dark. When the door was open, she stood aside to let him precede her. He hesitated, purely for reasons of politeness, and gestured to her to go first.

She hesitated in her turn over whether to insist, but decided against it.

"I'm not going to switch the lights on yet," she told him, as she stepped over the threshold. "You'll see why

214

in a minute. Your eyes have had time to adapt to the moonlight since we left the house, but a few minutes in Stygian darkness will increase the sensitivity a little more."

"I understand," Adrian assured her, as she closed the door behind him, cutting off the moonlight and leaving him momentarily in complete darkness. "I've already seen the direction of your work, from the painting of Jason onwards, all the way to Hell. I figured that the next step would probably be black on black, plus elusive shadows."

She laughed. "I knew you'd deduce the sequence, even though I deliberately mixed them up—another unnecessary test. So, have you worked out why I painted the pictures the way I did, rather than doing what a thoroughly sensible person like you would have done and gone into advertising?"

"I think so," Adrian said, patiently standing still and waiting for some guidance as to which way to move. "I suspect that you must have hoped, at one point, that your children might inherit your ability. When you painted Jason and the Fleece, you probably still thought that you might one day have an audience with whom to share . . . but genetics let you down."

He still couldn't see a thing, but he heard the movement of her arms as she sketched some sort of gesture. "They're as bad as Jason, poor lambs," she said. "I tried to teach them, to show them . . . but they didn't grow into it. They couldn't. Not their fault—entirely mine. I'd deduced from paintings, as you had, that there were people with some extra sensitivity, so I could have gone looking for them . . . but I wasn't thinking along those lines at the time, and I'm not sorry. The boys are better off taking after Jason."

She reached out then, and after a few seconds of groping, took hold his left wrist in her right hand.

"This way," she said. "You've seen Hell. Thus is what lies beyond—but you need to remember that it isn't quite finished. It's incomplete, in its fine detail. If I really thought that I'd ever complete it, perhaps I wouldn't be showing it to you . . . but I don't believe that I can, any more. Remember that too, and you might be able to think a little more kindly of me."

As she spoke she drew him, very slowly, along a short corridor. Then she said: "There are steps here. I'm used to them, but you'll have to be careful. There's a rail to your right."

He found the handrail. Still guided by her hand, he climbed the steps, one by one. Then there was another flat area. He didn't go far before she stopped him.

"This should be about right," she said. "I'm going to step away now. Don't move. It'll take me a minute or two, so be patient."

That was easier said than done. Adrian's mind was racing, trying to calculate exactly what, for Angelica Jarndyke, might lie "beyond Hell." As with the Rothkos in the Houston chapel, Adrian hadn't been able to see Angelica Jarndyke's depiction of Hellfire in a religious context—but he didn't think that mattered, because she had surely wrenched the imagery out of any specific dogmatic context, and restored it to a context of more primal fears. As he'd pointed out when confronted with the painting, you didn't have to be a Christian to understand the ideas of sin and guilt, and the imagery of eternal punishment; pagans could appreciate that just as well—and atheists too. Images of the Inferno could be unsettling even for people who didn't believe in God. That was, in a sense, the whole point of them.

Adrian had never hesitated for a moment over the explanation of his enhanced sensory perception. He had always taken it for granted that it was something natural, something explicable in terms of sense-organs, neurons and the properties of mind, something that bees could do. He had never thought of it as a kind of damnation, or a kind of curse. A freak he might be, he had realized, almost from the very beginning, but that was merely a matter of statistical oddity and genetic coincidence. He had always assumed that his special sight wasn't magic, even though he could see the elusive shadows, and every action he had taken in consequence of his perceived freakiness had confirmed and elaborated that conviction. He had explained himself, and he had set out to exploit himself.

He had never thought in any other terms than trying to market his knowledge, not just in the vulgar sense of making money from it but in the higher sense of a kind of artistry, of manufacturing beauty, of addressing an audience and supplying it with something subtle that would satisfy appetites that the brain had but that normal consciousness didn't know how to feed. For him, it had always been about color, and hence about light. Appearances, he knew, control attitudes, manipulate affections, and—ultimately—influence behavior. Clothes maketh the woman and man alike, and if people couldn't dress themselves to maximum effect then they had to look to others to help them out. The ability to manipulate the color sense of others subliminally was, in his view, *good*; the esthetic sensibility itself seemed to him to be good, because it would enable him to enable them to make the best of themselves. It was empowering. In pursuing the quest for Jason Jarndyke's Golden Fleece, and his own, Adrian had always believed that he was on the side of the angels, the side of *light*.

But for Angelica, he knew, it had been different; her ability had not led her toward the light, but toward darkness, not toward color but toward shadow, toward the liminal and the barely perceptible. For her the elusive shadows were and always had been the teasing essence of her exceptional sensibility. He understood now, never having had much reason to think about it before taking ship aboard the Airedale *Argo*, that someone else with his clear sight might easily have gone in a direction diametrically opposite to his, having been unable to accommodate the idea of uncanny sight to sensory apparatus, neurons and the capabilities of consciousness, but jumping instead to the conclusion that it was magic and witchcraft, even if only metaphorically, and hence a path of darkness and, ultimately, of doom.

As he had told Angelica a few moments ago, he understood the direction her painting had taken, as soon as the hope that her children might one day constitute an audience for it had faded away. She had become preoccupied, if not obsessed, with the project of occult painting, deliberately hiding imagery away from ordinary sight, of retaining it in her own possession, for her eyes only. But she had been aware, as he had, that there was a potential subliminal effect to what she was doing—that even people who couldn't see what she was painting could be unsettled by it, intimidated by the imagery, partly because they couldn't see it and partly because of what it represented: sinister imagery; menacing imagery; the imagery of witchcraft itself. And so, she had set out deliberately to unsettle and disturb.

There was a sense, Adrian suspected, that Angelica Jarndyke, a self-confessed unhappy woman in spite of her material wealth, had endeavored to paint curses. Believing that her art had the power to unsettle, she had decided to concentrate on that aspect of it, attempting to take it as far as she could. Had she believed that her power was literally magical, she might also have believed that she really did have the power to curse people by means of her paintings, but she was a child of the twenty-first century, and could only think of such notions in terms of symbol and metaphor. Even so, her curses might have worked, because color and its subtle variations really did have subliminal effects; appearances, including those not perceptible to quotidian consciousness, were capable of affecting attitudes, affections and behavior. The knowledge that Adrian was trying to use to empower people to make the best of themselves—or, at least, to empower Jason Jarndyke to sell them the means to make the best of themselves—could, in theory, be deployed to the opposite effect.

Mercifully, however, it hadn't worked, or had only worked in a very limited sense. At least, it hadn't worked on Jason Jarndyke, a man of very solid common sense, a man for whom a splodge was a splodge was a splodge. Perhaps, if Angelica had sought a wider audience, she might have had more effect on at least a few members of it, but instead, she had become increasingly introverted and isolated, imprisoned in her project. She had painted Hell, with little or no effect . . . and then she had tried to go beyond.

But how?

Where else but into the world of the elusive shadows, as she was able, willing and determined to imagine it?

He waited, impatiently, while she worked in the dark, perhaps made awkward by emotion even though she knew her way around the barn so well.

And then the lights came on.

They were by no means bright—indeed, they were exceedingly subtle—but there was still a momentary shock to his retina, and he blinked furiously for a second or two, struggling to readapt his eyes. It didn't take long for him. Within a matter of seconds he saw, vaguely at first, and then more precisely, and then as precisely as only he and Angelica Jarndyke could see, what she must have intended to be a kind of summation of her intellect, her experience, her dread, and her unhappiness: the elusive shadows of her paradoxical existence.

15

The murals were not confined to the walls; they covered the ceiling and the floor as well. There was, however, a surface area within the barn that represented a place outside the vision, a safe place to stand. Adrian realized that he was stationed inside a glass cube, enclosed within the volume of the building but deliberately set aside from it, as if in another dimension, albeit with windows allowing him to look in all directions, into all three dimensions.

The barn had a pitched roof on top, with exposed roof beams but the artist's artifice had abolished the angles; the space within the roof now seemed curved, and the entire configuration of the barn's inner walls seemed almost spherical. The viewer within the transparent cube did not seem to be standing on the bottom of something solid, even though he *knew* that he was on a glass plane looking through it at a further floor. Adrian could see the whole spectrum of colors, but when it came to the transparency of optically-perfect glass, he could still be fooled, and was still subject to illusion. The visual illusion was sufficiently powerful, at least at first glance, to cancel out the tactile awareness of the feet that he was standing on something solid. So far as consciousness was concerned, he seemed to be floating—and Angelica, who was standing between him and the entrance door, seemed to be floating too.

That illusion, rather than anything painted on the walls, made Adrian glad that Angelica was there—that there was something else he could see as well as the painted imagery. She, of course, had never had that advantage before—but she had built the illusion from scratch, highly conscious of its growth and development, and had spent most of her time outside the glass cube, working on the walls. She was not disconcerted; she was at home. She was not even looking at her own work: she was watching him.

Slowly, painstakingly, Adrian looked around.

At first he was slightly disappointed. He had not known what to expect, but, having followed his own train of thought, he had expected the extraordinary and the fantastic; he had expected, however vaguely, the conventionally monstrous. For a brief moment, as the images on the walls were resolved he felt that all his anticipations and anxieties had been deceived, that all his hypotheses had been mere fantasies. There was no Hellfire to be seen inside Angelica Jarndyke's vision of the world, no witches, no demons and no sinister mythological creatures. Nor, for that matter, were there any deceptive patches of primary color in which figures were lurking, outlined in subtle variations that most human eyes and minds could not discern, although there were several patches of seemingly-limitless darkness, of true unameliorated blackness, including a large rectangular section directly opposite the entrance door, suggestive of a tunnel or an abyss: a portal to oblivion.

Perhaps, Adrian thought, the paintings he had seen so far had only been one phase of her work; Angelica seemed to have moved on. She had used all the colors of the palette in decorating the walls of her barn, and had produced multiple images that Jason Jarndyke or anyone else with normal vision could have made out, and recognized. He would have been able to see a multitude of faces looking up at him, and a starry sky above him, and the horizons surrounding the enormous crowd, and the true blackness in front of him.

Jason Jarndyke would even have been able to recognize the expressions on the faces of the people in the painting—their superficial expressions, at any rate—and he might have been able to experience a strange vertigo in looking up at the sky and sideways at the distant horizons from within the glass cage. He might even have understood, without any prompting at all, why his wife had told him that her masterpiece was not a *Vita*, a compendium of human life in all its aspects. He might well have been able to understand, simply on the basis of what he could see, that it was quite the opposite: that this was a representation of human *death*, in all its aspects.

But he would not have been able to see all the detail of the depiction of death: not consciously. In fact, it took time for those details to emerge, even for Adrian's enhanced vision. Jason would not have been able to see the leering skulls within or superimposed on every agonized face. He would not have been able to see *into* the graves of the cemeteries filling the horizon. He would not have been able to sense, as clearly as Adrian could, that the blackness behind the stars really *was* absolute, that the space depicted really was infinite in its appalling emptiness, and that the stars themselves, even though they were supposedly distant suns, were merely futile flickering flames, helpless to stave off the empty dark, save for the illusions they created on the surfaces of absurdly small surfaces of orbiting planets, in the deluded eyes of the minuscule creatures swarming there. He would not have been able to get the true gist of the message.

And he would not have been able to see the elusive shadows, which even Adrian had not seen at first glance, so subtly were they depicted—but the longer he looked, the more he became aware of them, at least so long as he did not look at them directly. When he did, his first impression was surprise, because they seemed to be three-dimensional, although, being mere paint, they were not. Adrian realized that the impression of three-dimensionality was a *trompe l'oeil*, a trick of shading, assisted by the general diminution of light. As his eyes had adapted to what he was seeing, the monsters that had first seemed to be absent, and the quality of the extraordinary that had initially seemed to be limited, gradually came into view—*his* view, at least. But they first came into view peripherally, or liminally, and they too seemed three-dimensional, as if the wall were not a wall at all, but a continuation of empty space, essentially limitless.

How, he wondered, had Angelica contrived that curious effect? He did not know, but since she had been able to contrive it, it must be an exploitation of a peculiarity in human vision, a clever manipulation of the manner in which the eye and consciousness collaborated to synthesize the mental image of what actually existed out there in the noumenal world. It was not new; manipulation of the *trompe l'oeil* effect was very old, but its application here was particularly ingenious—and it made the elusive shadows, as Angelica had warned him, something other than what they seemed to be outside the barn, but something clearly related to the natural variety.

These elusive shadows were hovering above the people, in similar legions, like lesions in the air, distortions of the sky. They were not imagined in this depiction as the souls of the dead, nor as demons on the lookout for those souls. They were not predators and they were not tempters. Adrian had to grope for a concept by means of which to classify them, just as he had spent his life groping for a concept to classify the real thing.

They were "really" two-dimensional, of course, in the sense that all painted images are two-dimensional, but seen in this context, in this peculiar light, they had the illusion of depth: not solid depth but a deep concavity. They had the suggestive appearance of funnels in reality, whirlpools whose vortices extended to oblivion. Adrian understood now what Angelica had meant when she had told him that the elusive shadows seemed to her to be "hollow." They had nuclei of a sort, but not solid nuclei: voids like the center of a whirlpool, black holes toward which the eye was drawn by the numinous swirls around them.

Only a few of the elusive shadows were detailed, however; most were barely sketched. And Adrian realized that what he had initially mistaken for a deliberate vagueness in the crowd beneath was also an effect of the painting being incomplete, and that many of the human figures were also merely sketched. When—or if—all the detail was filled in, the effect of the skulls visible to him through the faces, and the effect of the elusive shadows that were invisible to ordinary human eyes, would be much more elaborate and much more intense . . . and the power of subliminal suggestion that it might exert on eyes that could not consciously see the elusive shadows would also be more intense.

The painting needed a space of this magnitude, Adrian realized, in order to acquire its full effect. It had to surround the viewer; it had to give the impression, not of a window, but a universe—*the* universe. It had to give an impression of a universe whose most fundamental feature, whose quintessence, was death. And here, in this representation, the elusive shadows were an aspect of death: not the souls of the dead preserved beyond the death of the body, even for the luxury of external damnation, but a face of death more ominous than a conventional skull: something sly and treacherous, but gripping and ineluctable, leading to the ultimate annihilation that was waiting in the wings to consume everything in the universe, and the universe itself.

In principle, Adrian supposed, the faces looking up at him had to be countable. There must actually have been a specific number, which could be calculated and recorded—but in terms of perception, in psychological terms, there was no way to number them. They were as many as all the humans that had ever lived and ever would, as different as all those human faces could be, and as similar. There were children among them, but none of them was truly alive; all of them were dying—not just the ones that bore the visible stigmata of torture and disease, but those that were seemingly healthy. He could actually see evidence of the truth that humans begin to die even before they are born, that they are sculpted by death and that death works within them.

Angelica had apparently come to the conclusion, after due experimentation, that supernatural imagery, stripped of its ancient contexts of belief, had lost its power to horrify. Even if she believed in her own witchcraft, she did not believe in the power of painted witches to terrify directly. She seemed to have come to the conclusion that she needed to go directly to the source of human *angst*, and all her subliminal imagery was calculated to appeal to that fundamental existential experience. Perhaps that was the substance of her curse—the curse she had aimed at anyone who might see her work without being able to see it all, and without being able to understand it, out of resentment at her isolation.

There was nothing insane about it—quite the reverse. It was supersane, aimed to corrode, undermine, and perhaps eventually to break down the most cherished illusions of the human mind.

Eventually, Adrian spoke: "It's not quite what I expected," he admitted, "But it *is* brilliant."

Then Angelica threw another invisible switch, and he realized that she had been playing with him. This time, the light was genuinely dazzling, more than momentarily—and when his madly blinking eyes had adjusted to it, he saw the remainder of the work.

The trickery of the inner cube was far more subtle than he had imagined; its transparency was manipulable. Now, thanks to the glass, Hellfire sprang forth to consume the dead, to wrench them from their rest, but not their pain. The red was superimposed on everything—and not just red, but all the subtle wrath of flame. And the black rectangle that had seemed to be a door to oblivion was now filled, with a self-portrait, of the face alone, detached from any body, and magnified to seven or eight time life-size, like a cinematic close-up.

It was a very accurate self-portrait. In fact, Adrian realized with barely a second's delay that it must actually have started out as a photographic reproduction, before Angelica had begun applying her expertise in make-up to its features. Perhaps she had, in purely literal terms, used an air-brush, but she had not been aiming to erase flaws in her skin exposed by the camera. She had been aiming for a different effect. She had been aiming for Morgan le Fay, Circe, Medea, or Medusa. Using nuances that the common eye could not see, she had made every effort to give her face the power to command, the power to curse.

Adrian felt his heartbeat accelerate, his thoughts reel. Momentarily, he felt the magic, and knew that there was a sense in which he was not merely as vulnerable to it as any other man, but more so.

The skulls and the elusive shadows were invisible again now. Only the first half of the dual image had been a symbolic representation of death. This was a representation of the other side of the coin: a very personal representation. This was the Hell of life, shaped by the awareness of death and its elusive shadows. This was the part of the work that constituted the true curse: the revelation calculated to seal the deal, to instill in the work's viewers the sharp blade of depression, the impaling dart of melancholia.

Adrian felt the infection sink into him, and he gasped—but then the consciousness of the scientist kicked in, as well as the consciousness of pure sight. He could see. He knew what was there, and what effect it was supposed to have on him. He could see it clinically as well as esthetically. He could analyze it as well as appreciate it. He was not required to react in purely emotional terms, or even with any emotion at all. He could do what he always did, and turn himself to metaphorical stone. He steadied his thoughts, and would have steadied his heartbeat too had he had the time to concentrate on relaxation. In fact, he let his heart race. It wasn't engaged in any other way.

"Holy shit," he said, eventually. "That's really something, Angie. You really have come a long way since you painted those studies in yellow and black, and even the study in red. This is a different order of magnitude altogether. It's genius."

"Would you advise me to finish it, then?" she asked. "To finish it and exhibit it."

"Absolutely not," he said, firmly.

"Why not?"

"Come on, Angie, you *know* why not. You've experienced depression. You've done your utmost to represent that depression. Doing that probably—undoubtedly—helped you to counter that depression, to diminish it, to give yourself the illusion of control over it. But precisely because you have experienced that depression, precisely because you know how closely akin it is to hell, it's the last thing in the world you ought to want to inflict on anyone else—especially Jason. I'm not saying that it would work on everyone, by any means, and maybe he's better armored than most to remain unaffected, but it's not a risk worth taking—not with him, and not with anyone."

"You seem to have come through it unscathed—and you can see it all."

"Yes I can—and that's why I know that it's a lie. That isn't what the elusive shadows are—although I'm very glad that you showed me that representation, because I might be able to get a better inkling now of what they really are, and perhaps a better hypothesis than all my juvenile fantasizing about a two-dimensional parallel universe overlying the surface of the earth. But what's more important, from your own point of view, is that this isn't what *you* are. The depression might make you feel like that, sometimes, but you know full well that the depression isn't you, Angie. You're better than that, and you're far more than that. That's not the person I see when I look at you, and it sure as hell isn't the person that your husband sees. The objective, surely, isn't to make the rest of the world see you and themselves as you see yourself at the worst moments of your delusion, but to help you see yourself as they see you when you're at your best, and to help them see themselves in the same way. That's what constitutes the good, morally as well as esthetically. And you don't need me to tell you that."

Angelica Jarndyke flicked the second switch again, and the room went dark—completely dark so far as Adrian's unadjusted eyes could see.

"Actually, Adrian," she said, quietly, "I did, just as I needed you to tell me . . . to convince me . . . that the monsters lurking in the walls of the world were actually real, simply natural phenomena, not aspects of my madness . . . or the world's. You're right, of course—it is a lie. I thought it wasn't, at first, but it is. I shouldn't finish it—not as it is. I need to rethink it, rework it, make it better. It'll take time . . . a long time . . . but as Jason is so annoyingly fond of saying, life's a marathon, not a sprint."

Adrian carefully refrained from mentioning Plutarch. Instead, he said: "Thank you for showing it to me. It *is* a work of genius. But . . . as you say, it could benefit from reworking. In the meantime, make sure you keep the door locked, and don't ever let your children steal the keys. Do you think we should go back to the house now? We've been away longer than the half hour you promised."

"Don't worry," she said. "Jason won't make a pass at Meryl, and he won't bore her to death either, even if he rabbits on about his blessed textile exhibition. The only danger is that they'll finish off the brandy. I'll have to switch all the lights off to open the cage, though. Stay where you are, and I'll come and lead you back to the door."

Mention of the brandy reminded Adrian that he was still holding the glass; he hadn't touched a drop since he had entered the barn. He took a careful swig while he waited to be collected.

When they were outside, she said: "I didn't start out wanting to inflict my depression on other people by subliminal suggestion. I just wanted to use the painting to get a clearer view of myself, to see whether I could analyze my unhappiness. I have kept it all to myself, you know—I've never tried to exhibit it. You were a special case. I'm not a monster. I got carried away with the exploration, but I don't think I would ever have finished it, and if I had, I would have kept it to myself."

"I know," he said. "But you wanted me to underline that conclusion, so I did. No offense intended."

"None taken," she assured him. "You've just told me that I'm a genius, and, coming from the only person in England, perhaps in the world, who's qualified to make the judgment, that means something. As for the rest, you did exactly what I wanted you to do." She sighed before adding: "Men always do."

They paused at the back door and looked around. There were no elusive shadows visible now; the one that had disappeared was presumably still holed out wherever such shadows went, if they went anywhere at all.

"I'm sorry that you're unhappy, Angie," Adrian said, feeling that he ought to say something. "I wish I could tell you how to be happy, but the mere fact that I'm happy myself, for the moment, certainly doesn't make me an expert."

She had her hand on the doorknob, but she didn't turn it immediately.

"Are you *sure* we're not just crazy?" she asked. "That's it's not just a case of *folie à deux?*"

"Perfectly certain," he said. "We just have a sensitivity that's normally the prerogative of bees and hummingbirds—something that enables us to make clothes worthy of emperors that street-urchins can't comprehend. It's a gift. It's just a matter of figuring it how to use it. We've had our problems, but on the whole, we're not doing that badly, are we? And we have the whole future ahead of us in which to do even better."

16

"Adrian and I have a confession to make," said Angelica to her husband, almost as soon as they had rejoined Jason and Meryl. Meryl, who was half-expecting some such announcement, and was somewhat relieved to hear it, merely smiled. Jason looked appropriately horrified, but he succeeded in not believing the inference he had been momentarily tempted to draw, and managed to content himself with saying: "Oh?"

"Actually," Angelica added, "that's badly phrased, *I* have a confession to make. Adrian has only become involved recently, entirely innocently, but he's the one who has enabled me to make it. I've been keeping a secret from you, Jason, for fifteen years, but I can tell you now."

"Oh?" said Jason, again.

"The enhanced vision that he and I possess doesn't just allow us to discriminate shades of color that other people's eyes can't make out. It also allows us to see . . . things . . . entities . . . what Adrian calls elusive shadows. Neither of us could ever be sure that we weren't just seeing things, until we were able to compare notes and ascertain that we really were seeing the same thing, that the entities really are there, and weren't it a product of our diseased minds. We met in secret last Monday in order to do that, and we've now been able to confirm that our experiences match, at least approximately. I'm truly sorry for deceiving you, Jason, but I was frightened. I've always been far too close to being certified crazy for my liking, and I didn't dare risk drawing the lightning down. Now that Adrian can confirm that the elusive shadows really do exist, and aren't delusory, I feel a great deal better. It doesn't solve all my problems, by any means, but it has helped a lot. We're sorry that we went behind your back, but it really was in a vital cause. I needed him to see the barn just now for the same reason. I *have* been a little crazy, but thanks to him, I think I might be able to make progress now, back to a higher degree of sanity and stability."

Jason Jarndyke shook his head, but not in denial. "You could have told me," he said. "I would have believed you."

Angelica smiled, thinly. "I didn't want you to have to make the effort," she said.

The Industrialist's gaze shifted to Adrian. "So what are these things you can see?" he demanded.

"Actually," Adrian confessed, "I'm no longer so sure that they are *things*, as such. I was, until half an hour ago, but I've just seen something in the barn that has given me pause again. At least, it's suggested a new idea."

Angelica was now looking at him as well, and he had never seen her gaze so intense, or so demanding. "What do you mean?" she asked.

"We might have been making a mistake, Angie—both of us, for a long time. We've both been assuming that we were in an either/or situation: that either the elusive shadows were real entities existing in the world around us beyond the reach of ordinary vision, or that they were the product of delusion, and hence a symptom of some kind of worrying mental disturbance. Your use of the *trompe l'oeil* effect to give your painted shadows the illusion of a third dimension suggested to me that the ones we see out there in the world might share an analogous combination of real existence and illusion. Your painted images are actually two-dimensional, but appear scarily three-dimensional, like hollow funnels drawing the eyes into a kind of void. The thought occurred to me that perhaps your models are the other way around—that they only appear to be two-dimensional, while actually being three-dimensional—except that their third dimension doesn't extent in our three-dimensional manifold, but in another."

"I don't understand," said Angelica.

"Nor do I," said Jason Jarndyke.

Meryl said nothing, but Adrian guessed that although she was struggling with the idea, having already been introduced to the inclination of his thinking, she was not making much headway either.

"It is odd, admittedly," he said, soldiering on regardless, "but it might help explain how the elusive shadows disappear. The two-dimensional world in which they seem to exist might actually be a planar intersection between two three-dimensional universes that overlap, as it were, with the result that a three-dimensional object

236

in one manifold appears in the other as a two-dimensional cross-section, and when the object moves in its own world it can move out of that plane of intersection entirely, thus disappearing from view."

"I think I see what you mean," said Meryl, trying to be helpful, "but it doesn't explain why the object disappears when you look directly at it."

"Not in itself, no," Adrian agreed. "But it does open the question of what kind of object it is that is being protruded through the intersection—and, if the protrusion is deliberate, why."

"You're back to monsters from the nth dimension," Meryl suggested.

"In a way, yes—and also the notion of the elusive shadows of lenses of some kind. And the monsters aren't monsters, but merely observers, perhaps endowed with a special kind of vision, and the nth dimension is merely a third dimension—just one that doesn't happen to be ours."

"But if that's true," said Angelica, "than the elusive shadows, or what lies beyond them, really are lurking, lying in wait, and *watching* us?"

"Perhaps, but I don't think so—and this applies to all the hypotheses I've come up with, not just the new wrinkle. I've given the matter some thought over the last week. Perhaps they *can* see into our world, somehow, but they can't really *enter* it—all they can do is skim its surfaces, intangibly. They seem very reluctant to approach us, or come into our buildings, but even if they were to become more audacious, I don't think that they could possibly hurt us. It seems to me that they're simply curious, and deeply puzzled about a reality that might well seem exceedingly bizarre and alien to them.

"At any rate, I now think that my teenage self was wasting his time and theirs by trying to stick them with darts, when what he should have been trying to do was figure out a way of sending them signals, with a view to opening up a channel of communication; one-way to begin with, but eventually, who can tell?"

"Are you serious?" asked Meryl, incredulously.

Adrian was about to shrug his shoulders, and say that it was just another hypothesis, but Jason Jarndyke intervened before he could make the gesture.

"Of course he's serious," the industrialist said. "He's a genius. I don't understand a word of what he said about dimensions, but I know that it isn't just hot air, or he wouldn't have said it. If anyone else told me that something was picking holes in our world with some kind of thingamajig in order to watch us through the hole, I'd think they were suffering from paranoid delusions—but when it comes from Adrian Stamford, I know it's at least worth serious consideration.

"And when Adrian has just spent the last hour, not to mention last Monday night, making careful observations in the company of my wife, who has the same special sight as him, I'm even more inclined to take it seriously. It might take me some time to get my head round his hypotheses, but I'm willing to bet that they're not baseless, and I know that before he risks any definite conclusion, he'll make every effort to check it out thoroughly.

"That's why I hire geniuses: they take things seriously. That's why I know that I'm going to get my Golden Fleece, eventually . . . and who knows what else, as he keeps on having bright ideas along the way. He even makes Angie feel better—which, believe me, is a Herculean feat. So let's for God's sake sit down and have another drink, and stop getting all steamed up about irrelevancies."

The master had spoken. Obediently, they all sat down, and Jason filled the empty brandy glasses. Then he took Angelica's hand, and squeezed it. He didn't make a further speech specifically to her, but he communicated to her easily enough that there was nothing that needed to be forgiven, and that to the extent that matters were in his dependency, she had nothing to worry about. She thanked him in the same mute manner.

"So all that stuff you fed me last Friday about bumpy flatlands and their strange inhabitants was just fantasy after all?" Meryl said to Adrian, in a low voice.

"I never said it was anything else," Adrian replied. "It was the fantasy I liked best at the time, and it's still as likely to be true as any other—but that was then and this is now, and I've complicated my thinking a little."

"That was the day you said you loved me—and swore to me that it would last at least till today."

"That hasn't changed," Adrian assured her. "Believe me, nothing that Angie showed me in her barn has shaken that conviction. It's just given me more food for thought regarding other matters, just as I've given her some food for thought. That's good, from everybody's point of view."

239

He looked at Angelica in search of an endorsement, and this time he got one, with a firm nod of the head. She was convinced, at last, that he really was an ally—and all her intimidating hurdles had now been taken.

If Jason Jarndyke was surprised to hear Adrian calling his wife "Angie" he made no comment. He contented himself with taking an appreciative swig of brandy and saying: "I am right, aren't I, in thinking that everything *is* all right now? As well as can be expected, at least."

"Better than that, Jayjay," his wife assured him.

"Amen to that," said Adrian, raising his glass and glancing at Meryl.

"Never better," she assured everyone, raising her own glass. "Long may it last."

"Here's to art and artifice, then," said Jason Jarndyke. "May we see the Golden Fleece in my lifetime."

And they drank to that.

17

Adrian had hardly started working at his terminal the next morning when Jason Jarndyke appeared beside his desk.

"I don't suppose there's any chance of you telling me exactly what you saw in the barn last night?" he asked. "Angie won't tell me. So much for not having any more secrets."

"I can't," Adrian told him. "In any case, when the painting's finished, it will look quite different. She told me that she's going to scrub out some of the images and replace them."

"But you did tell her that it's a work of genius?"

"I did," Adrian agreed. "But I also told her that I didn't really like it. She wanted me to be honest. I don't think she was upset. She'd already decided to rework it. She only wanted confirmation of her own verdict. Because I could actually see the hidden part of the work, I was the only person who could give her that confirmation, but it was just a rubber stamp. She'd already made her decision"

"You didn't actually like *any* of her stuff, in fact, did you? None of the ones you saw at the house?"

"I quite liked the one of you."

"There's one of me?" Jarndyke's expression brightened.

"You're hidden in a yellow splodge, but I could see you . . . with the Golden Fleece. That one's a happy one. You could safely hang that, if you wanted to."

Jason nodded. "Perhaps I will," he said. "She's not happy often, poor lamb. I do my best but . . . you know that people around here call her Medea, don't you?"

"It's just a joke, because Jason and Medea were married."

"But it's not a very nice joke, is it? Do you know how the story ends?"

"Nobody does—there are half a dozen different versions."

"But the differences, so far as I can tell from my web searches, are all to do with the fate of the children. The mythical Jason always dumps Medea for a new trophy wife. I'm not going to do that. I'm not that kind of man."

"I know that. So does Angelica. So does everybody else, really. You mustn't take superficial jokes too seriously—or mythology, come to that. They're just stories, more often slanderous than not. For all we know, the real Medea was actually a model wife and Jason a paragon of husbands, who loved her to his dying day. You mustn't take Euripides seriously. And in any case, you and I are probably the only people in the building who have even heard of Euripides, except for Horst Koerner . . . and as he says, outside of their specialties, the rest can't tell Mozart from mozzarella. All they know is that

Medea was Jason's wife. That's the entire foundation of the joke."

The Industrialist shook his head, ruefully. "I've been doing her a serious injustice all these years, you know," he said. "I really thought there was nothing there, that it was all bluff. I didn't like her painting at all. Made me feel quite uncomfortable at times, although I have no idea why. I'll try to make it up to her, if I can."

He could have gone away then, but he didn't. There was something more he wanted to say, but he was having trouble spitting it out.

"I have been in the barn, in fact," he confessed, eventually. "I couldn't resist the temptation. Angie would kill me if she knew, but I had to. I had to try. I saw the things I could see: the faces, the red light, the self-portrait. I didn't understand it, because I never do understand that sort of thing, but it did seem very clever, with that glass box and all. You saw more than me, though, didn't you? There are things hidden in it that I can't see—that I'm not meant to see—aren't there?"

"Yes, there are," Adrian confirmed.

"If I knew what they were . . . would I be worried? Should I be worried?"

"I don't think so, Mr. Jarndyke," Adrian told him. "To tell the truth, I was a little worried myself, beforehand . . . scared even . . . but that was silly. As you say, it's very clever. Very clever indeed. Your wife is a real artist. She still has a lot of future ahead of her."

"You won't tell her I've seen it, will you?" the industrialist said, anxiously.

"Your secret's safe with me," Adrian assured him. "All your secrets are safe with me."

"I took a risk hiring you, you know, Son. Not with respect to coloring the fabrics—it was blatantly obvious that you were the man for that job, and I'm extremely glad that I got to you ahead of the opposition—but with respect to the other thing. I didn't know whether you were going to see anything at all, and I still don't know what it is you saw . . . but I did know that it would make a difference, either way. That was a risk."

Adrian nodded, to show that he understood.

"I'm happy," the big man told him, out of the blue. "I've always been happy. I'm a happy man. Maybe it's because I can't see things that other people can, and maybe I'm just made that way. I'd really like Angie to be happy too, if that's possible. Do you think that's possible, Adrian?"

"I don't know," Adrian admitted. "I'm the last person in the world who can offer an opinion on that matter."

"You might think that," Jason Jarndyke said, "but I don't believe that it's really true. I could tell, remember, that you needed to get out more, to get a girl-friend, to have some fun. I was right, wasn't I?"

"Yes."

"And I fixed you up with the ideal woman, didn't I—for you, that is?"

"Absolutely ideal. Don't get me wrong—I couldn't be happier. I just don't think that that entitles me to give anyone else advice on how it's done. It was all done *for* me, you see, by you and by Meryl. I didn't have to lift a finger. Mind you, I'm not at all sure that it's in your interest for me to be happy. It's surely best for you and Jarndyke Industries for me to be single-minded, obsessive, and utterly committed to the quest for the Golden Fleece. If you want to surround yourself with happy people, you could just as well hire idiots. If you want to make trillions . . ."

Jarndyke cut him off with a dismissive wave of the hand. "I don't hire happy people," he said. "That would be silly. I hire geniuses—but then I do my best to make them happy. It's not easy, God knows, but when it works, it pays off. Trust me, Son. I know what I'm doing."

"I do trust you, Mr. Jarndyke," Adrian said with a smile. "I think you're a genius too, in your way. You're a man who has everything, after all—and it wasn't blind luck or a helping hand from others. You've *earned* everything, including happiness. Not many people can say that."

"Bullshit," said Jarndyke, although he didn't mean it, and it wasn't true. Again, he could have left on that note and let Adrian get back to work, but again, he didn't.

"If you're right about these elusive shadows that you and Angie can see," he said, "is there any way of making money out of it?"

"I don't know," Adrian told him. "Not immediately. But if there really are other three-dimensional manifolds capable of intersecting ours, and ways of opening windows of some sort in the intersection . . . well, it's probably a billion-to-one shot, but it would at least be interesting to find out. Who can tell? There might be entrepreneurs over there making billions out of the things they learn from spying on us . . . but probably not. I really don't have much time to devote to that sort of investigation—but if you wouldn't mind me collaborating with Angie, I might be able to work out a program for her to follow, if she's interested. Between the two of us, given time, we might eventually be able to work out exactly what the damn things are."

Jarndyke nodded. "I'll ask her," he said. "I wouldn't do it for anyone but you, mind."

"Because I'm the only man you trust not to try to seduce your wife?"

"No—because you're the only man in the world that I couldn't bring myself to kill if you did." Jason Jarndyke laughed, because he thought it was a joke. Then he became serious again. "I still want you to tell me what you saw in the barn, though," he said, a trifle plaintively. "I want you to explain to me what it was that you saw but I couldn't."

"I can't," Adrian told him.

"Because Angie forbade you to?"

"No, because I literally can't. Sometimes, you have to be there. Sometimes, it just isn't possible to explain what I can see to people who can't see it for themselves. I'm sorry."

Lying, Adrian thought, wasn't as difficult as it sometimes seemed—and sometimes, it wasn't all that difficult to keep the story straight, even when the reasons were tangled.

"She still won't let me in, you know," Jason continued. "You're very privileged—and she doesn't hold it against you that you didn't like it. She told me this morning that you were a real treasure, and that I should be sure to cherish you. She said she wished that she could do what you can do. We can't all be scientific geniuses, though, can we?" He sighed, and almost turned away, but then remembered that he really shouldn't be calling in at his employees' labs just to talk about his wife, mythology and art. "How are things coming along, then?" he asked, in an ostentatiously business-like tone, in order to transfer the dialogue back to safe ground, to the *terra firma* of biotechnology.

"The deeper reds are beginning to come along nicely, confirming the accuracy of the cyberspatial molecular modeling. The next set of test genes is ready for implantation for preliminary trials. The true blues are slow—but organic chemistry's always had difficulty with true blues. I hope to have the first of the lemon yellows ready for implantation next week . . . but I still haven't got a handle on the configuration of the perfect gold. I'll know it when I've imagined it, because it will be the most beautiful DNA sequence in the world. It's just a matter of racking my brains, and reaching out a little further . . . eventually, I'll find it."

"It's a marathon, not a sprint," the big man said, automatically, presumably not as familiar with Plutarch as he was with Euripides. "Making progress—that's the main thing."

"It's the only thing," Adrian replied. "It's all we really have, this side of the grave. All else is illusion and elusive shadows."

A PARTIAL LIST OF SNUGGLY BOOKS

G. ALBERT AURIER *Elsewhere and Other Stories*
CHARLES BARBARA *My Lunatic Asylum*
S. HENRY BERTHOUD *Misanthropic Tales*
LÉON BLOY *The Tarantulas' Parlor and Other Unkind Tales*
ÉLÉMIR BOURGES *The Twilight of the Gods*
JAMES CHAMPAGNE *Harlem Smoke*
FÉLICIEN CHAMPSAUR *The Latin Orgy*
FÉLICIEN CHAMPSAUR
  The Emerald Princess and Other Decadent Fantasies
BRENDAN CONNELL *Unofficial History of Pi Wei*
BRENDAN CONNELL *The Metapheromenoi*
RAFAELA CONTRERAS *The Turquoise Ring and Other Stories*
ADOLFO COUVE *When I Think of My Missing Head*
QUENTIN S. CRISP *Aiaigasa*
QUENTIN S. CRISP *Graves*
LADY DILKE *The Outcast Spirit and Other Stories*
CATHERINE DOUSTEYSSIER-KHOZE *The Beauty of the Death Cap*
ÉDOUARD DUJARDIN *Hauntings*
BERIT ELLINGSEN *Now We Can See the Moon*
ERCKMANN-CHATRIAN *A Malediction*
ENRIQUE GÓMEZ CARRILLO *Sentimental Stories*
EDMOND AND JULES DE GONCOURT *Manette Salomon*
REMY DE GOURMONT *From a Faraway Land*
REMY DE GOURMONT *Morose Vignettes*
GUIDO GOZZANO *Alcina and Other Stories*
EDWARD HERON-ALLEN *The Complete Shorter Fiction*
EDWARD HERON-ALLEN *Three Ghost-Written Novels*
RHYS HUGHES *Cloud Farming in Wales*
J.-K. HUYSMANS *The Crowds of Lourdes*
J.-K. HUYSMANS *Knapsacks*
COLIN INSOLE *Valerie and Other Stories*
JUSTIN ISIS *Pleasant Tales II*
VICTOR JOLY *The Unknown Collaborator and Other Legendary Tales*

CPSIA information can be obtained
at www.ICGtesting.com
Printed in the USA
LVHW041729140920
665974LV00009B/1336